Christmas Journeys

*Christmas is a magical time of the year,
a time for happy gatherings with loved ones to
celebrate the festive season...no matter how
far we must travel to be with them!*

*With these four brand-new stories, we invite
you to share the sparkle and excitement of
yule-tide romances, impromptu kisses under
the mistletoe, chance meetings and unexpected
marriage proposals. Join four delightful
couples as they journey home for the
holidays—and discover the true meaning of
Christmas...that love is the best gift of all!*

About the Authors:

EMMA RICHMOND was born during the war in north Kent when, she says, "farms were the norm and motorways non-existent. My childhood was one of warmth and adventure. Amiable and disorganised, I'm married with three daughters, all of whom have fled the nest—probably out of exasperation! The dog stayed, reluctantly. I'm an avid reader, a compulsive writer and a besotted new granny. I love life and my world of dreams, and all I need to make things complete is a housekeeper—like, yesterday!"

CATHERINE GEORGE was born in Wales, and early developed a passion for reading, which eventually fuelled her compulsion to write. Marriage to an engineer led to nine years in Brazil, but on his later travels, the education of her son and daughter kept her in the UK. And instead of constant reading to pass her lonely evenings, she began to write the first of her romance novels. When not writing and reading, she loves to cook, listen to opera, browse in antiques shops and walk the Labrador.

LYNSEY STEVENS was born in Brisbane, Queensland, and before beginning to write she was a librarian. It was in secondary school that she decided she wanted to be a writer. "Writers, I imagined," Lynsey explains, "lived such exciting lives: travelling to exotic places, making lots of money and not having to work. I have travelled. However, the taxman loves me dearly and no one told me about the typist's backache and frustrating lost words!" When she's not writing, she enjoys reading and cross-stitching, and she's interested in genealogy.

KAY GREGORY grew up in England but moved to Canada as a teenager, and now lives with her husband in Vancouver. They have two sons who have recently moved away, along with two ferrets, leaving them sole custodians of the family dog. Kay has had more jobs than she can possibly remember, the best of which is writing romances!

Christmas Journeys

EMMA RICHMOND
CATHERINE GEORGE
LYNSEY STEVENS
KAY GREGORY

Harlequin Books

TORONTO • NEW YORK • LONDON
AMSTERDAM • PARIS • SYDNEY • HAMBURG
STOCKHOLM • ATHENS • TOKYO • MILAN
MADRID • WARSAW • BUDAPEST • AUCKLAND

CHRISTMAS JOURNEYS

Copyright © 1994 by Harlequin Enterprises B.V.

ISBN 0-373-15271-X

CHRISTMAS JOURNEYS first printing September 1994

The publisher acknowledges the copyright holders of the individual works as follows:

A MAN TO LIVE FOR
Copyright © 1994 by Emma Richmond
YULE TIDE
Copyright © 1994 by Catherine George
MISTLETOE KISSES
Copyright © 1994 by Lynsey Stevens
CHRISTMAS CHARADE
Copyright © 1994 by Kay Gregory

CONTENTS

A MAN TO LIVE FOR

Emma Richmond

Chapter One

WAITING. A little bit nervous, a little bit sad. Hair beaded with moisture, coat damp. A new situation, a new beginning. T'was the night before Christmas, and all through the house... Hardly appropriate, she thought with a tiny smile, although it *was* the night before Christmas, but here, at eight o'clock, staring out through the window of the VIP lounge in the Gare de L'Est, *everything* was stirring, including, no doubt, a mouse. French, of course. And amid all the bustle, the laughter, the tears, one little tableau stood out, drew the eye. A beautiful woman, elegant, exciting, voluble, Francine thought with another small smile, not that she could hear what she was saying, only see the movement of that red-lipsticked mouth, and register the utter immobility of the very impressive-looking man she was talking to. A man to die for. Tall, good shoulders, dark hair going grey. Late thirties, she guessed. A face that was impassive to the point of derision. Intriguing. And expensive. Oh, yes, definitely expensive, as were the people behind her, people who *belonged* in a VIP lounge.

The gentle touch on her arm startled her, and she turned, stared into the smiling face of the hostess.

'We are ready to board,' she told her softly. 'The porter will take your luggage. If you will follow him?'

With a nod, she relinquished her suitcase into the care of the porter in his distinctive red coat and cream gloves, and followed him from the private lounge towards the train. I'm here, she told herself, in Paris, and about to board the exclusive, and astronomically expensive, Europa Express. Alone. Renowned worldwide for its cuisine, its luxury, Francine fought to accept a fact that felt like fantasy. To have actually *been* on the Europa was to be—famous. And yet, the train seemed shorter than she would have expected. Only four carriages. Sleeping compartments, lounge, dining-car, and kitchens. Plus engine, of course.

With one last look at the busy station, at the magnificent Christmas tree that dominated its surroundings, at the man to die for, she climbed aboard—and stepped back in time. Old wood pannelling, brass fixtures and fittings, dark red carpet, an ambience of age. Edwardian splendour. She was taken to her beautifully appointed cabin, assured that she only had to ring for anything she might need, told that champagne, or tea or spirits, or anything else she might like, would be waiting for her in the lounge, and was then left alone to unpack, savour the beginning of her journey through some of Europe's most spectacular scenery. A journey given in love, which should have been shared.

Pushing the sadness aside, and the slight feeling of intimidation her surroundings gave her, she washed and changed into her wickedly expensive little black dress, courtesy of her beloved godmother who had insisted on buying, and overseeing, her wardrobe for the trip, stared into rather wistful brown eyes, and forced herself to smile. Yet for a moment, another image was superimposed over her own, grey hair drawn back in a chignon, faded blue eyes, one lid lowering in the suggestion of a wink before her own image came back, her own cloud of nut-brown hair overshadowing the ghostly image of Marie Louise, her godmother, her beloved Mally. Enjoy it, she had said, if not for yourself, then for me. Yes, she would enjoy it for Mally.

Too thin by her own estimation, but tall and elegant to anyone else, chin tilted just a little bit defiantly giving her face a rather severe beauty, she made her way through to the lounge bar. Her friends always insisted that she looked arrogant, self-possessed, and a snob. Those who weren't her friends presumably didn't like to. It was being tall, and slender, these helpful friends decided, and the aquiline nose, which gave her a haughty expression. Hardly comforted by these revelations, and deciding that going round with an inane grin on her face wasn't even to be thought of, at the age of twenty-eight, she decided that people would just have to take her as they found her. But if she looked self-possessed, even if she didn't feel it, that was all to the good among a group of people who were probably born that way. Better to look haughty than nervous.

Pausing in the doorway, she smiled at the incongruous sight of a grand piano at the far end, exchanged nods and smiles with the people nearest her, and grateful for the attention of a smiling steward, accepted a tall fluted glass of champagne. Feeling a little less nervous, she glanced from the window as the train began to move, and her mouth twisted humourously as people on the platform turned to stare curiously at the distinctive train, then wave, as though it was a good thing, a nice thing for people to be so fortunate. And so it would have been, if Mally had been with her.

Hearing a small stir behind her, an accent that seduced, she turned—and found herself staring into the face of the man to die for. The man from the station. And just for a moment, her heart gave a funny dip. Kismet. Don't be silly, Francine.

Unsmiling, he gave a brief nod, then turned to the
couple on his right. They spoke in French, and although
she was fluent in the language, she didn't really listen,
just watched him, the economical gestures he made as he
spoke, the way he tilted his head. Aloof, a barrier deliberately erected between himself and the world. A devas-
tating man, and although no emotion showed, she got the
feeling he was angry about something. As he moved to
greet someone else, his arm caught hers and he halted,
stared at her as though expecting her to apologise, and
when she merely tilted her chin, gave him back look for
look, he made a brief, dismissive, gesture, murmured,
'Pardon,' in a voice that cut, and moved on. Arrogant.
Wealthy. A man used to getting his own way. A cut
above. None of which excused bad manners. Perhaps he
was important. Perhaps people always apologised to him
first, whether it was their fault or no, but she didn't know
these people, didn't mix in these circles, and she didn't
really know the form. Did one casually circulate? Or
continue to stand in isolated splendour awaiting recog-
nition? Seemed a bit pathetic—and Mally would have
been furious. Mally had told her to have a good time.
Looking up, she found one or two people watching her,
and was quite unaware that she was the main subject
under discussion, that speculation about her was rife.

A little gong sounded, and conversation stopped. The
steward smiled, and informed them that dinner was
about to be served. They were shown into the dining-
room, and Francine sat alone at a table that should have
been shared. Mally should have been sitting opposite.
Mally with her wicked tongue who would have reduced
these fine looking people to the mundane. Mally, who
had never been intimidated in her life. But it was a little
odd that they all seemed to know each other.

'*Vous permettez?*'

Startled from her introspection, she glanced up at the man to die for, and felt that same sliding feeling in her tummy. Automatically answering him in French, she whispered in astonishment, 'You wish to sit with me?'

'Naturally.'

Naturally. 'Why naturally?' Her voice emerged in a husky croak, and she hastily cleared her throat. 'Not five minutes ago...'

'I treated you with contempt? Yes.' Sliding into the seat opposite, he regarded her with sombre grey eyes. Waited.

Feeling slightly unnerved when she should have been furious, she told herself, yet not knowing quite else what to do, she extended one slim hand. 'I'm...' she began.

'I know who you are,' he interrupted dismissively. 'Why are you here?'

Puzzled, and not knowing why it was any of his business, or how he knew who she was, she said coolly, 'Because I was asked.' No, told, she mentally corrected. As she had been. Mally had made her promise, in fact.

He gave her a considering look, which just bordered on offensive, and drawled in perfect English, 'I wonder why?'

Her back stiff, hackles rising, she switched easily to her native tongue. 'Presumably, because I was wanted. The ticket is all bought and paid for.'

'Paid for?' he queried.

'Yes. Well, not by me,' she added honestly, 'but certainly by *someone.*'

'Ah, yes. Someone.'

Beginning to get extremely annoyed, and unconsciously adopting the look that was the despair of her friends, she gave him an arctic smile. 'Do you know,' she began conversationally, 'how infuriating it is to be echoed?'

'No,' he denied bluntly.

No. Presumably no one ever dared to echo him, and he was beginning to make her feel like the poor relation, and that made her cross, and when she was cross, she tended to do things she shouldn't. She'd felt as fine as five pence until she'd walked into the lounge and seen the gowns the other women were wearing. Expensive to her was obviously merely a rag to them, and now here was this superior being, trying to make her feel even worse. Why?

'You don't know who I am?'

'No,' she denied as bluntly as he had. 'Should I?'

'Not necessarily. I'm Giles Lapotaire.'

Jeel, she mouthed to herself, and smiled, because it was a nice name, a name that conjured up the best of the French. What a pity his mother had had such a lack of insight.

'It is amusing?' he asked softly.

'No.'

'Ah.'

Ah? What did that mean?

Alerting the waiter with an impressive flick of one finger, a gesture that, used by most people, would be open to misinterpretation, because only a few, a very few, could manage it without giving offence or appearing rude, he ordered a bottle of champagne, and when it was open, glanced at her for her approval, an unconscious courtesy, and when she nodded helplessly, filled both their glasses, then silently saluted her.

She echoed the gesture, then added quietly, 'A journey into Christmas.'

'Yes, a journey into Christmas. And for the next few days, we will be—exciting strangers on a train.'

He spoke as though conferring a favour, and her mouth tightened fractionally, yet perhaps the arrogance, like the courtesy, was unconscious, part and parcel of the way he was, and wasn't meant to be offensive. Oh, yeah? And maybe oranges were blue.

'Are *you* exciting?'

'Never,' he denied.

'Never?'

'*Non.*'

'And I thought all Frenchmen were exciting.'

'Or only hoped?'

'Perhaps hoped,' she agreed sweetly.

'Then here's to hope.' Raising his glass, he toasted her. 'And I am Swiss, not French,' he corrected. 'And it is a well-known fact that the Swiss are very, very, unexciting.'

Were they? Sardonic or ironic, she wasn't sure which, and he'd only been a man to die for until he'd opened his mouth and let loose his cutting comments. Now he was a man to kill. Or definitely severely injure, so perhaps the elegant lady on the station had been justified in her volubility. Feeling very unlike her normal friendly self, forced into behaving in a way that was foreign to her, like a haughty little madam who knew the ways of the world, she moved her eyes to the pink-shaded lamp that shed a rosy glow across the snowy damask tablecloth, sparked off the exquisite silver cutlery, and sighed. 'Do you often take instinctive dislikes to people?' she asked quietly.

'Meaning you?'

'Of course meaning me.'

Watching her for a few moments in silence, relaxed, in perfect command, he finally murmured, 'It wasn't instinctive.'

'Not? Then why?' she asked in bewilderment. 'Or are you normally this rude?'

'Probably,' he agreed indifferently.

'But you do dislike me,' she persevered.

'Yes.'

'Why?'

'Isn't it obvious?'

'No.' Looking up, she said quietly, 'No, it isn't.'

'Then I will tell you.' Accepting the tasselled menu and wine list from the steward on her behalf, he continued, 'Because Marie Louise was a friend of mine.'

Startled, she echoed, 'A friend of yours?'

'Yes. She was special. One of the old school. An autocrat, who mistakenly always put her family first.'

Despite the fact that they didn't deserve her consideration. Well, she couldn't argue with that. Her daughter had been impossible, and her grandaughter, Cecille, was even worse. Did he therefore assume that her goddaughter was of the same ilk? Obviously he did.

'Order your meal.'

Her mouth pursed, she accepted the menu from him, and barely registering the delicious fare, quickly ordered.

'She wrote to me before she died,' he explained quietly.

'Did she?' Not quite sure what response was required of her, she waited helplessly.

'Yes. To say that she would be unable to come.'

'Unable?' A puzzled frown in her eyes, she added, 'But she...'

'Didn't know she was going to die? She knew, and told me that it was to be my good fortune to take care of you on the journey.'

'Good fortune?' she exclaimed with a very unhumourous laugh. 'A strange way of putting it.' And he certainly didn't look, or behave, as though it was his good fortune, he looked as though he thought it was a chore. In which case... 'How fortunate, then,' she told him in the same kind tone that grated only slightly, 'that you will have no *need* to take care of me. I am so very good at taking care of myself.'

'I know.' Not even bothering to look up, he continued his perusal of the wine list.

Mouth tight, she glanced at her fork, nobly restrained the impulse. Serious, attractive—rude. The sort of man she would never have met in normal circumstances. The sort of man who moved in circles far removed from her own. All the men wore evening dress, yet his not only clung, but seemed to lovingly caress those broad shoulders and deep chest, and his shirt, unruffled, was of the finest, softest linen, the shot cuffs discreetly fastened by gold links, the hands square, long-fingered, bare of rings. Unmarried? Glancing at his face, she admired the symmetry. Deep sockets, clear grey eyes, finely marked brows, a determined chin, arrogant nose, and a mouth made for passion. So silly to be attracted by looks alone, yet women often were.

He glanced at her, did not look away. Folding the wine list, he handed it to the steward with his decision, nodded dismissal, linked his hands together, and continued to watch her. Confident, assertive, very much aware of his own masculinity. As was she.

'You were her lawyer?' she guessed. He looked as though he would be very good at interrogation, at legal matters.

He shook his head. 'Banker. Very dull, very boring. Very—unexciting. And you are a...' Thoughtfully tilting his head to one side, he pronounced, 'Socialite.'

'Socialite? No.' Is that what Mally had told him? Dear Mally, who had never quite understood what she did. Or approve. 'No,' she repeated. 'I do whatever needs to be done. An—innovator, if you like.'

'Explain.'

No smile, no invitation—had she expected one?—just that one explicit order. Abrupt. And deciding that to be angry with him would be a waste of emotion, she answered in the same quiet tone he was using. 'I make things people need.'

'Such as?'

With a little shrug, searching for an example, she murmured, 'If, say, you needed a particular type of tie-pin and didn't know where to find it, I would offer to find it for you, or failing that, make it.' Lifting her lashes, she watched him watching her.

'A tie-pin.'

'Yes. Or a hat-pin for Great Aunt Alice, or a dress or a shawl, a lacquered cabinet, a replacement piece for your favourite chess set. Something different, something special, something—unobtainable. How many times have you heard someone say, "I wish I could find such and such." Or, "Do you have any idea how hard it is to find a so and so?"'

'And so you go up to them and offer?'

'Yes.'

'Solicit,' he murmured.

'No!'

His shrug was better, more—eloquent.

'I do not solicit! And whether you believe me or not, making things is what I do. A scourer of junk shops, a detective of memorabilia, a finder of the unfindable.'

'In other words, you get the glory and someone else gets the grime.'

Not understanding, she frowned at him. 'I don't know what you mean.'

'Don't you? Never mind. Tell me why.'

'Why I do it?'

'Yes.'

'I don't know why I should tell you anything,' she argued pithily, 'but I do it, because I can. I trained in design, fashion, I used to make things for my friends, and then friends of friends, and when I graduated, discovered that competition for the few jobs available was so fierce, I continued to do so, just to mark time. And when I have nothing to make for other people, commissions, I make things to sell on market stalls, local shops...'

'And never did get to work in one of the fashion houses,' he stated. 'And do you make a living from these—innovations?'

'Enough to make me happy.'

'And what constitutes happiness?'

'Enough money to pay my bills, buy my food, to be decently shod and clothed, have enough left over at the end of each month to make me feel—worthwhile. To have someone to laugh with, love with, friends who view life as I do, see as I see, or if they don't, to have the wisdom not to beat me over the head with their own ideals.'

'And you also love old ladies, children and animals.'

'Don't sneer.'

'Why? You expected me to believe you? I told you, I knew Mally.'

And Mally had told him—what?

'And do you have someone to love with at the moment?'

'No,' she denied baldly.

He gave an odd smile. 'No,' he agreed musingly, 'no more do I.' The little toast he gave her was ironic. And not in the least understood.

'Giles?'

A scarlet-taloned hand descended onto his shoulder, a blonde head appeared beside his, and he lazily turned his head.

'Marguerite.'

'What have you done with Claire?' she demanded.

'Should I have done anything?' he asked dismissively.

'Well, she isn't dining with you!'

'Obviously.'

'Don't be difficult! Is she in her cabin?'

He didn't answer, merely stared at her with hooded eyes, and with a little tut, she removed her hand, tossed her head and walked towards the sleeping-carriage.

His face expressionless, his voice equally so, he mused, 'I wonder why I invited her?'

'Perhaps for the same reason Mally invited me!' she returned waspishly.

'Perhaps.'

'And how come everyone knows you? Knows each other?'

Eyebrow raised at her accusatory tone, he proposed, 'Because we are all—friends?'

'*All?* Oh.' A group booking. 'And Mally knew them, too?'

'Some. Not all.'

'Oh,' she repeated thoughtfully. Well, that explained a few things.

'Inquisition over?' he asked sardonically.

Eyeing him with dislike, she shrugged. 'For the moment. Is yours?'

He nodded, got to his feet. 'Enjoy your meal.'

'You aren't eating?'

'No.' Raising the wine glass he still held, he mockingly toasted her. '*Bon appétit.* I've chosen a wine I think you will appreciate.' Replacing his wine glass on the table, lids veiling his eyes, he added very, very quietly, 'Cause any trouble, and you're off the train.'

With an outraged gasp, she exclaimed, 'Trouble? I never cause trouble!' Embarrassed, because it had come out louder than she'd intended, aware that people had turned to look at her, she glared at him. 'What has Mally told you?' she demanded.

'Enough.'

Her mind racing, she blurted, 'Well, it couldn't have been anything terrible, because I haven't *done* anything terrible.'

'No?' With another considering little gesture which was beginning to infuriate her, followed by the inevitable shrug, he agreed, 'No, perhaps not by your own interpretation.... However, if you could manage to stay away from the married men,' he murmured silkily, 'I would be extremely grateful—but do join us in the lounge when you're ready,' he invited blandly. And then his mouth quirked in almost humourous derision as he added, 'I believe there are to be—jollifications.'

'Oh, goody.'

And this time he did smile. It even reached his eyes. Turning away, he nodded to one or two people as he made his way to the far end of the carriage, and out of sight.

'Mademoiselle is ready for her soup?' a polite voice enquired.

No, mademoiselle was not ready for her soup! Mademoiselle was ready to spit nails! Snapping her head round, she forced her mouth into the semblance of a smile, then leaned back, allowed the steward to place it before her. 'Thank you.' And if her voice sounded gritted, hopefully he wouldn't notice. Picking up her spoon, she held it like a dagger. What an unutterably fool thing to say! She supposed that little barbed reference had been because of Edward. But she hadn't *known* Edward was married. Not until his wife had knocked on the door, and then she'd been as shocked as everyone else. But why had Mally told Giles? Because it must have been her that had done so! She had told her godmother in confidence! And Mally had been so very angry, she remembered, and had naturally thought the anger had been directed at Edward, but now it seemed that it had been directed at herself. And what else might she have told him? Every little incident in her life? And for why?. Because he had been her confidante? Yet how often had they met? She'd stayed with her godmother many, many times, and *she'd* never met him. Never even heard him mentioned. And anyway, Mally rarely saw anyone these last few years. Said she was too old for socialising; very rarely even went *out!* Had remained in her villa just outside Nancy, and any commissions were executed by either her housekeeper or Francine, when she'd been there. Did he work in Nancy? Despite being Swiss, as he'd so pompously told her. Mally's bank manager? And then she scowled to herself. Giles Lapotaire was nothing so mundane as a manager. More likely, he owned the bank! Although she understood now why Mally had *written* to him, but why had she never told *her* it was a group booking? That everyone would know each other? And had she really known she was going to die?

Automatically eating her meal, she continued to puzzle over Mally's behaviour. Certainly she'd been astonished when Mally had proposed it! Worried that it would be too much for her, and for someone who never went anywhere, to suddenly decide to take a long train journey through Europe, no matter how exclusive the accommodation might be, had seemed extraordinary enough, but if she had known she was dying, why had she booked it at all? Because she had wanted Francine to go on it? And had known that she wouldn't have gone on it without her godmother? It seemed very convoluted. But Mally must have had *some* reason in mind. Mally had never done anything without a reason!

When the last dish was removed and coffee brought, her speculations no nearer finding a solution, she sat pensively watching her fellow travellers for a little while. Only about twenty or so, which again surprised her. She wouldn't have thought so few passengers would be a viable proposition. However, it must have *been* profitable, otherwise the owners of the train wouldn't have done it.

People with money, she thought, still watching them, who had wanted to do something different for Christmas. And tomorrow night, a grand party at an exclusive hotel in Chur, then, possibly, onto a different, but equally sumptuous, train, for a journey into the interior because the gauge of the railway was different, or something. Francine didn't quite understand all the ramifications, only knew the timetable, which might change, her itinerary informed her, due to the weather, the mood of the train driver, rulings of Swiss Federal Railways, or an Act of God.

And did Giles's behaviour come under the heading Act of God? Probably, she thought morosely. Finishing her coffee, she returned briefly to her cabin to tidy herself, a cabin that had been transformed into sleeping quarters, and glancing from the window, saw that the sleet had turned to snow, and as the train rushed towards the Swiss border, the darkness began to lighten with the glow of patchy white fields, which would soon give way to a wholly unrelieved snowy blanket. A white Christmas. Glancing at her watch, she saw that there was only another hour to go before it would be Christmas Day. Her first Christmas on her own. No, that was foolish, she wasn't on her own, but she wished with all her heart that Mally could have been here. Wished she could just go to bed!

When she returned to the lounge, hair brushed, lipstick renewed—hauteur in place, she thought with a sigh—she halted in the doorway, and involuntarily smiled. The tree had been lit, red candles placed safely around the perimeter of the carriage, and with the overhead lights dimmed, they flickered cheerfully in their sconces, and suddenly, it *seemed* like Christmas. But Christmas was a time for families, and she didn't have one. Oh, don't be so pathetic, she scolded herself.

An elderly American couple entered behind her, exclaimed in delight at the transformation, and Francine turned to smile at them. They smiled back, and suddenly, everything seemed better. Someone to smile with, someone to say hello. Because of Giles's behaviour she had been in danger of misjudging them all. And most of them *were* nice, she discovered. During the next few minutes, she was gently reprimanded for eating alone; offers were extended to join this person or that, drinks brought for her, and slowly, as people began to relax, mix, began to lose their inhibitions, as the pianist began to play, Francine put aside her bewilderment and tried to enjoy herself.

There was a goodly mix of French and English spoken, the odd phrase in German as people tried to find a common denominator; laughter and hesitancy as people got muddled switching from one language to another, and as Francine idly listened, joined in when she was spoken to, danced when she was asked, her eyes searched the room for Giles Lapotaire. Surely he was intending to join them? How could she flirt with all the married men if he wasn't there to *see,* she wondered tartly? Although judging by the derisive way he'd mentioned the jollifications, perhaps not. Perhaps he was in his cabin reading. Scowling over customers' overdrafts... And then she saw him enter, and still angry from his jibes, she gave a rather wicked little grin. He certainly looked as though he'd been scowling over something, and now she could give him something else to scowl over. He should have remembered that people like to live up to their labels. Especially women.

Glass in hand, he moved from group to group, spoke a few words with each, distantly, judging by his expression. Perhaps he was warning them about the Jezebel in their midst. He should meet Cecille, she thought, then he'd *really* know what a Jezebel was like. And when he'd finished circulating, as though he were the *host,* he stood quietly watching, a faint smile on his face. Not a smile of enjoyment, more derision, as though for a species he didn't in the least understand, was merely tolerant of. And then she saw Marguerite, also scowling. She caught Francine looking at her, and walked over. Looking her up and down, she gave a cold smile.

'Hardly tasteful,' she remarked rudely, and ignoring the gasps of Francine's companions, continued, 'So where is she?'

'Who?'

'Claire.'

'I have no idea.'

She gave a disbelieving snort. 'Well, you won't last. You aren't his type. And had it been a public train, one could almost have been forgiven for thinking you'd wandered into the wrong section.' Without waiting for a comment, she walked away towards the piano, then leaned, supposedly seductively, within the curve—and Francine burst out laughing. She couldn't help it, the exchange had been so absurd.

'I don't think I have ever...' the American lady began in outraged tones. 'Europeans are supposed to be so *mannered!*'

'Most of us are,' Francine soothed, the laugh still in her voice. 'As are all well brought up people, no matter where they come from. We will just have to suppose she wasn't brought up very well.'

'But what did she mean about taste? You look lovely.'

'But not designer,' Francine murmured.

'Well, if she's designer I'd rather have Woolworths!'

With a splutter of laughter, she gave the woman an impulsive hug, then turned when she heard the laughing commotion from behind her. As in parties everywhere, wherever they were, whoever they were with, hats and streamers were always produced, in this instance by a lady called Anise. She took no notice of anyone's refusal to make a fool of themselves. *Everyone* she insisted, would wear a hat, including Giles—and everyone laughed. Why, Francine wondered?

Po faced, he refused the pirate hat she was offering, and, face still expressionless, he delved into the box she was holding, and produced a crown. His face was impossibly bland, but amusement danced in his eyes as he placed it solemnly on his head.

'*Bon Noel*, Anise.'

She curtsied, and continued on with her box, and when everyone was hatted to her satisfaction, except for Marguerite, Francine was amused to notice, she beamed impartially, instructed the pianist in his repertoire, and insisted everyone mingle. Her current companions were dragged off towards a nearby group, and Francine thrust willy-nilly into another, then immediately dragged to one side by a grey-haired gentleman with twinkling blue eyes. He had the most delightful accent.

'Everyone is asking who you are, and obviously too polite to ask, but *I* intend to find out! Are you, or are you not, an interloper?'

'An interloper?' Francine echoed in astonishment. 'Is that what everyone thinks?'

'Of course. A lady of mystery. Who *are* you?'

A rather naughty smile playing around her mouth, and suddenly aware that Giles was watching her, she said softly, 'An interloper, of course. Are you um, married?'

His smile was slow, appreciative, as though he understood her very well—or thought he did. 'Would it matter?'

'Yes.'

'Why?'

She grinned, then chuckled deep in her throat, an unconsciously provocative sound she was quite unaware of. 'Because I only flirt with married men. *Only* flirt,' she emphasised, then gave him a meaningful little glance under her lashes to make sure he understood.

'Ah. And only in full view of... *Non, non, non,*' he exclaimed, laughing, as Anise tried to drag him away, 'I am just in the middle of...' But it did him no good, even without Anise, because the revellers shifted and she was absorbed into another group whether she wanted to be or not! Laughing, still able to see her new friend's frustrated expression, she found herself pressed up against the bar. The wind was getting up, she suddenly registered, and glancing at one of the uncovered windows, saw that snow was beginning to pile against the frame, and she gave a little shiver.

'A fortunate intervention,' Giles drawled softly from behind her. 'And very bad psychology on my part.'

Swinging round, she stared up into his face, felt that funny little dip again, almost a squirm in her tummy, and wondered why he hadn't told anyone who she was. Natural enough, surely, to explain that Mally's goddaughter would be on the train in her stead. 'Disastrous,' she agreed sweetly. 'And I didn't even get to find out if he was married.'

'He is.'

She smiled, and hoped it looked as feline as it felt. She would have to practise, she decided, in the privacy of her cabin. She would get rid of the haughty look if it killed her and become the *femme fatale* he so obviously thought she was. And he would never know how much of a joke *that* was. Ever since that nasty little episode with Edward, the only *fataling* she'd done was to her neighbour's cat!

'And his wife is—here?'

'No. And don't even think about it.'

'Or else?'

'Most definitely.'

Practising her smile, and admiring the crown that still sat proudly on his arrogant head, she asked softly, 'Who's Claire? The lady on the station?'

He merely smiled.

'Just wondering, you understand, seeing as *everyone* keeps mentioning her.'

'Then wonder silently.'

'Have a row, did you?' They'd looked as though they'd been having a row. No, *Claire,* if indeed it was Claire, had looked as though she were having a row. Giles had just looked impassive. Much as he looked now. And he'd said, hadn't he, however sardonically, that he had no lover at the moment. Which presumably meant... 'And why,' she continued naughtily, 'is Marguerite so anxious to find her?'

'Because she's lost?'

Giving in reluctantly, she changed tack. 'Then tell me why everyone defers to you. Keeps telling you how wonderful it all is.'

'Because I invited them?'

'*Invited* them?'

'Yes—apart of course, from you.'

'Yes,' she agreed sweetly, 'apart, of course, from me. And you haven't told them who I am, have you? And now they seem to think I'm an interloper.'

'Do they?'

'Yes! So why didn't you tell them? Correct any misconceptions?'

'Because it amused me not to?'

Yes, she could well believe *that!* 'And if you invited them, presumably paid for them?'

He nodded.

'Then you can behave any way you choose?'

He gave another of his infuriating smiles.

'It must have cost you a fortune!'

'Then how fortunate that I have one,' he agreed blandly. 'Your glass is empty, do let me have it refilled.' Summoning the barman, he exchanged her empty glass for a full one, and then continued, 'I do assure you I haven't been rifling the bank's funds...'

'I never assumed you had.'

'Or hijacked the train, merely hired it.'

'*Hired* it?'

'Yes, I dislike entertaining, you see.'

'Dislike...'

'Entertaining,' he repeated helpfully. 'And shopping for Christmas presents. This seemed a good way of, er, killing two birds with one stone. Repay in one go all the hospitality I have enjoyed during the past year, and not returned—until now.'

Not entirely sure she believed him, but incredulous none the less, she stated, 'You hired a train, paid for all these people because you dislike buying Christmas presents, and are now stuck with them for a week because you hate entertaining?'

'Ah, but I shan't be with them for a week. I shall be leaving the train at Weesen. *I* am going skiing. Disappointed?'

She shook her head, sipped her fresh glass of wine. 'Relieved,' she murmured—and then really registered what she had said. Paid for them. Including, presumably, Mally. And Mally had... Snapping her head up, she stared at him in shock. 'You paid for *me?*'

'No need to look so alarmed.'

But she was alarmed. She didn't want him to have paid for her. 'I thought it was a gift from Mally,' she said worriedly.

'And so it was. She wanted you here, and here you are.'

But *he* hadn't wanted her. Bought and paid for. 'You invited Mally, and then Mally asked if I could come...'

'Ask? No, Mally did not ask. And if you knew her as well as you say you do, you would *know* that. Mally only ever informed.'

Yes. As Mally had informed her that she would be coming on this trip. Mortified, she murmured stiffly, 'I see. No wonder you were...'

'Leave it,' he instructed, and he sounded bored again, dismissive.

But she couldn't leave it. She didn't want for him to have paid for her. And she didn't know whether to be angry with Mally, or him. 'I thought Mally had booked it, paid for it as a present... I didn't know,' she repeated stupidly. Pride flooding her, she tilted her chin. 'I'll leave at the next main station we come to.'

'We aren't stopping at any main stations,' he informed her blandly.

'Then I'll...'

'Don't be absurd. You will stay—and behave yourself.'

Was his voice warmer? Amused? And why wasn't she *insisting?* Perhaps she was still a little numb—or perhaps, a nasty little voice whispered in her mind, his looks, his charisma, her reluctant reaction to his magnetism, cancelled out his abominable behaviour. Behaviour that now made a little more sense. Although many women, she imagined, would forgive this man a great deal, and it had nothing whatever to do with his undoubted wealth. Although it was probably his wealth that had made him the way he was. And the truth was, she didn't want to leave the train. Found she was beginning to enjoy crossing swords with him. It made her feel alive. Something she hadn't felt in a long while.

And then he smiled. Quite a nice smile, actually, and she began to wonder what he was *really* like.

'You aren't *quite* how I imagined you.'

'Aren't I?' she asked artfully.

'No.' But he didn't explain *how* he had imagined her. There was another gust and the train tilted slightly, throwing her off balance, not enough to make her fall, only stagger, and he easily caught her, steadied her—and then left his arm round her.

She gave him a speculative look, and he smiled again—derisively. It became even more derisive when a dramatic flourish of chords were struck on the piano.

'Ah, I believe that indicates that we have reached midnight, and the beginning of Christmas Day. Carols will be sung,' he informed her solemnly, and her lips twitched.

'Good King Wenceslas?' she asked tongue in cheek with a significant glance at his crown.

'Quite possibly. I believe Anise has also organised games. And the only game *I* play,' he added in soft warning, 'is golf.'

'And you not even married,' she murmured naughtily.

'No, which is the way I intend it to stay.' And with the season's greetings ringing out around them, accompanied, she saw, by a great deal of laughter and kissing, he bent his face close to hers, and with a rather wicked smile in his eyes, whispered, 'Happy Christmas.'

And then he kissed her. Thoroughly. Expertly, devastatingly. Shook her to the core. Shocked, because she hadn't expected a kiss to feel like *that,* she drew back, stared at him, her breathing uneven. Say something, she urged herself as her eyes remained locked with his, anything to make the moment go away.

'And did the earth move for you?' she quipped raggedly.

'No,' he denied eventually, 'only the train.'

Chapter Two

RELEASING her, he gave a mocking smile, sauntered away, and was lost from sight as he was absorbed into another group.

'At last!' someone exclaimed from beside her, and she turned to find the man with twinkling blue eyes—twinkling at her. Her smile abstracted, she fought to pull herself together, and she did try, but flirting had suddenly lost its appeal. Thankfully, the noise and the laughter gave her a good excuse to pretend she was unable to hear him, and deciding that enough was enough, she mouthed, 'I'm going to slip away—alone,' she insisted when he gave a roguish smile. 'I've been up since six this morning, and it suddenly seems to have been a very long day.'

'For sure,' he agreed, 'and is likely to get even longer.' With a gentle smile, he captured her hand and raised it to his lips. 'I will wish you good night, sweet lady, and thank you for your charming company, but tomorrow, ah, tomorrow is definitely another day—and I am very determined.'

With a chuckle, she released herself and fought her way towards the exit. It didn't stop her being kissed, or hugged, wished Merry Christmas by those she passed, both male and female, and she forced herself to respond, enter into the spirit of the thing, but it felt like hard work now, not enjoyment. Although pride, and

Giles's rather sardonic observation of her, acted as a necessary spur.

Finally reaching the doorway, she slipped through and made her way along the swaying carriages to her cabin. Leaning back against her door, she stared at nothing. It was only a kiss, she tried to tell herself, but it wasn't true. It hadn't only been a kiss. It had been a deliberate assault on her senses. Why? If he disliked her as much as he said he did, why kiss her at all? She couldn't even tell herself that her reaction had been because of tiredness. True, she had been up early, but then, she often was. And the drive to Gatwick, the flight to Paris, hadn't been that long. She'd been stuck in traffic jams in London longer than that. Perhaps it was the residue of the emotional upheaval caused by Mally's death. But she knew that wasn't true, either.

Had he been at the funeral, she wondered? The final goodbye that Francine had been unable to attend because of a severe dose of flu? Had that been a black mark against her? Her nonattendance? Which brought her back to why he had kissed her. As punishment? But it hadn't been a punishment, had it? With a long, deep sigh, she straightened, began to prepare for bed. All the men she had kissed, either in fun or loving, not one of them had ever made her feel like that. And it wouldn't go away. Just thinking about it brought back the same feeling. The same churn of excitement inside. And she was only here because he'd paid for her. The only uninvited guest. Why, Mally? she asked silently. Why did you insist I come?

Disturbed, worried, she lay in the narrow bunk and idly listened to the faint sounds of revelry, the occasional burst of laughter, and felt isolated, which was foolish, but gradually, the sounds of the train, the rhythm of the wheels on the track, began to soothe her, until, suddenly, out of the blue, came an echo from the past. Faint, because it had been such a long time ago, her father's voice, and the silly little rhyme he'd made up on another train journey when she'd been small.

Fields slipping past, hear the wheels on the track. Adventures ahead, there's no going back.

Odd to remember that now. Feeling sad and rather wistful, she stared out at the dark night. He could never have known how prophetic his words would be. She could even see his face, the warm, comforting, smile, the fun in his eyes as he'd made up the little rhyme to amuse her. She'd been eight years old, travelling to Scotland for a holiday—a holiday that had never even begun, because the next day, he was dead of a heart attack. Had gone on the biggest adventure of them all, and she'd fervently hoped that he'd met up with her mother, in heaven. Her mother who'd died when she was born. Mally had said he had. That he was happy now. And so had begun another adventure, with Mally, in France. And now her beloved Mally was dead—and she was no longer a child.

She woke at five, not knowing where she was for a moment, then relaxed, glanced from the window. Still dark, but with that eerie, exciting glow that snow makes. Christmas Day. Happy Christmas, she whispered to herself. And she was thirsty. The wine, she supposed. And once you wake up and your body tells you it's thirsty, there is absolutely no going back to sleep. The mind insists on a drink. *Her* mind insisted on orange juice. Her body wanted some vitamin C. Lying there, trying to convince herself she didn't want any such thing, she determinedly shut her eyes, then sighed. She could almost taste it, anticipate the cool freshness ... Oh, knickers.

Shoving the cover aside, she slid out, padded into the tiny wash cubicle and peered at herself in the mirror. Yuck. Splashing cold water on her face, she cleaned her teeth, dragged on her dressing gown, pushed her feet into her slippers, and cautiously opened her door. Subdued lighting lit the corridor, glowed softly on all the closed pannelled doors, and hesitating only a moment, she padded softly towards the lounge. Dreamlike, diffused lighting bounced off brass fitments, silvered the cords of the window blinds—and then she became aware of the soft notes of the piano, felt a little shiver go down her back at the evocative tune someone was picking out. *Für Elise.* Beautiful and haunting.

Humming softly to herself, still moving quietly, she peeped into the lounge. Giles. Tie undone, jacket slung round his shoulders gangster fashion, face impassive, slight stubble darkening his chin, he continued to pick out the notes one handed, unaware of his audience. He looked—lonely. That mouth touched mine, she thought with another little shiver, a shiver of remembered pain and pleasure, of shock. It had moved on hers with deliberation, and she felt again that frisson of desire that had raced through her, the warmth that curled her toes, the spiralling pain inside—and she wanted to feel it again, that special ache, that feeling she had never felt before. That—ignition.

He looked up suddenly, trapping her, and she blushed, felt a fool. To retreat would be an admission of intimidation, and so she stepped forward, managed a mocking smile. 'Happy Christmas.'

He nodded, continued to pick out notes.

'I was thirsty.'

'You should have rung for a steward.'

About to tell him that she hadn't liked to, she changed her mind. Sophisticated young women of the world who ran off with other people's husbands *always* rang for stewards. Or so she assumed. Not being an expert on the subject, she decided to keep quiet. Walking across to the bar, she helped herself, hesitated. 'You want one?'

He shook his head.

'You haven't slept?' Silly question, Francine. Does he look as though he's slept?

'I'll grab a few hours in a minute,' he murmured absently.

'Nice tune.'

'Mm.' Lifting his hand, breaking off mid tinkle, he carefully closed the lid, glanced at her. 'You weren't at the funeral,' he stated baldly.

'No.' Funny he should mention that when she'd been thinking the same thing not so long ago herself.

'None of her family were.' An accusation. Failure to do what was right.

'Were you?' she asked quietly.

'Obviously, otherwise I wouldn't have known you weren't.'

'Not necessarily, someone might have told you.'

He shrugged.

Sipping orange juice she no longer wanted, she said quietly, 'I loved Mally very much.'

'Did you?' he asked indifferently, 'Then you had a funny way of showing it.'

'How would you know? You never saw us together.'

'True.'

'And hearsay is inadmissible evidence.'

His smile was brief, very faint, and totally unamused. Hitching his jacket more firmly onto his shoulders, he rose, gave her a look of studied indifference, and walked out.

Had he thought she was being facetious? She wasn't, and he didn't have the right to judge her. Feeling depressed, she waited until he'd had time to gain his cabin, then slowly followed. She tried to get back to sleep, but the little exchange with Giles kept going round and round in her head. And if she'd told him she'd had flu? What then? Nothing, he probably wouldn't have believed her. A fair trial was obviously beyond his comprehension.

At seven, the motion of the train somehow different, she got up, went to look from the window. Coming into a town. Geneva. Headquarters of the World Health Organisation, and the Red Cross. Bordered to the north by the Pays de Gex, and south, the Haute Savoie. It was beginning to get light, and she could just make out the silvery sheen of the river. The Rhône, she remembered. Cornavin Station slid by in a rumbling blur, and then they were picking up speed again as they ran through the outskirts that looked like the outskirts of a town anywhere. Versoix, Coppet, light gradually spreading over the countryside as they thundered towards Lausanne. The lake would be on her right, Lake Léman, cold and deep, frozen? And she shivered suddenly, feeling cold.

She showered in the small cabinet, the hand-held equipment awkward but adequate, then rubbed herself briskly with the thick warmed towel provided. Taking her time, because she obviously had plenty of it, she pulled on new lacy underwear, and a bright red dress which had seemed smart and appropriate when she'd bought it, but now, she thought, looked ridiculous. All she needed was a long white beard and a sack of toys... Staring at herself, she gave a wry shrug, then a little chuckle. This won't do, she told herself. Mally said you were to enjoy

yourself, and had apparently told Giles that it was his
good fortune. Well, let's see how much good fortune we
can throw his way, shall we? Forget the fact that he paid
for you. Forget the kiss, the impact he has—on probably all females from birth to death—and go down
fighting. You come from a long line of fighters, my girl!
She didn't know if she did, but it sounded positive. And
if he wanted to be rude, well, then, let him. No need for
her to descend to his level. She hadn't invited *herself*,
that's what she must hold on to. Hadn't deliberately *en-
croached!* In which case... And after this trip, she was
never likely to see any of them again.

Collecting her make-up bag, she carefully laid out all
the necessary equipment and set to work. Half an hour
later, she stared at herself, began to giggle, then shook
with silent laughter. She looked like a vamp. A carica-
tured one, at that! Toning it down slightly, she blotted her
scarlet lipstick, widened her eyes, then thoughtfully tilted
her head to one side. It definitely needed something else.
Seeking inspiration, she peeped out into the still-empty
corridor, although she could at last hear signs of stirring
from the other guests, and her gaze lit on an arrangement of poinsettias twined artistically round a lamp
bracket. With a naughty smile, she carefully broke off a
flower and hurried into her compartment. Pinning it
above her left ear, she admired the effect. Perfect. Very
dramatic. Just like Carmen Miranda!

Black shoes, black bag, black and red scarf, she walked
out, head high. Still fighting her grin, she strolled along
the corridor. A steward was walking towards her carrying a tea tray, and as he glanced up, he started, grinned,
hastily straightened his face, then grinned again—and
gave a little snort. Her own smile very, very wide, she
asked happily, 'Outrageous?'

He bit his lip, nodded.

'Good. A very happy Christmas to you. I smell coffee.'

He pointed to the lounge, and she sailed majestically through, accompanied by his splutter of laughter.

The steward serving coffee had better training, or certainly better control over his facial movements, and only the tiny widening of his eyes betrayed him. She grinned, struck a pose, and he smiled. 'Bon Noel, mademoiselle.'

'Bon Noel,' she returned solemnly.

'It is a joke?' he asked hopefully as he took in the full splendour of her appearance.

'Certainly it is a joke.'

'Ah, *bon*. Coffee? Champagne? Bucks Fizz?'

'Coffee, please.' Peering at his name tag, she added warmly, 'And may I say that you have the most delightful accent, Jean-Marc?'

'*Merci,*' he thanked with a little inclination of his head. Offering her a seat with a dramatic flourish, he snapped his white napkin across one arm, placed her cup before her, and carefully poured. 'Such *magnifique* deserve—*homage,*' he concluded proudly.

She inclined her head, and he smiled. 'If you can't beat 'em, join 'em, isn't that what they say?'

'I believe it is so,' he agreed solemnly.

'And so, today, I thought I would cheer everyone up. Become a talking point.'

'You already are,' Giles drawled from the doorway.

'Only because they don't know who I am and you refused to enlighten them,' she scoffed.

'As did you? Coffee, please, Jean-Marc.'

Jean-Marc bowed and went to get him a cup whilst Giles came to sit opposite her.

'I shall not rise,' she warned him calmly. 'Today, I am immune.'

'Hm.' Viewing her magnificence with a sardonic smile, he leaned forward for a closer look at her patently false eyelashes, which had *not* been bought for this trip, but had lain forgotten in her make-up case since a fancy dress Hallowe'en party she'd attended. But finding them this morning, and deciding that more was definitely better than less, she'd carefully applied them. Whether they would last the day without falling off was another matter. She smiled seraphically at him.

'You look like a...'

'Tart? Yes, I know. But I felt the dress was a mistake, and with mistakes, you either have to bury them or enhance them. I decided to enhance.'

'Burial might have been better,' he argued softly. Quietly thanking Jean-Marc for his coffee, he picked up his cup and sipped, eyeing her over the top. As she eyed him. He'd presumably showered, and most definitely shaved. His chin was nice and smooth, and the faint aroma of a no doubt expensive aftershave wafted towards her. He was wearing a very nice Italian knit shirt, and jeans.

'You didn't dress up,' she reproved.

'No, I viewed your magnificence earlier when you desecrated the flower arrangement outside your cabin, and knew I could never compete,' he said drily.

'I didn't see you.'

'I know. Happy Christmas, for the second time.'

'You didn't wish it the first time.'

'I thought it,' he said even more drily, and she smiled, remembered his kiss, and felt sad.

What would it be like to be loved by this man? To be even *liked* by him? 'Was Claire meant to come?' she asked without even knowing she was going to, and his face changed, became closed.

Looking down, she stared into her coffee. 'I saw you on the station.'

Silence.

Looking up, she pulled a face, changed the subject. 'What did Father Christmas bring you?'

'He hasn't been yet. Trains are always last on his list. A final rest for the reindeer before they fly back to Lapland.' Cocking his head momentarily, glancing briefly towards the roof, he observed softly, 'I think I just heard them land.'

'Fool,' she reproved and was unaware of her wistful smile.

Finishing his coffee, he got to his feet, stared down at her for a moment, as he had the day before in the dining-car, then gave a quirky smile, unutterably appealing. 'Your daisy's wilting.'

Automatically putting up her hand, she felt it, fixed it more firmly, and reproved, 'It's not a daisy. It's a poinsettia.'

'Whatever, it's still wilting. Excuse me, I have to go and put out the sherry and mince pies.'

She frowned, then realised what he meant. For Father Christmas and his reindeer. Not that she supposed he was doing any such thing. It had merely been an excuse to leave. But her parents had. She clearly remembered the ritual with the stockings, the excitement when he'd been. But not Mally. Mally hadn't believed in sentimentality, as she called it, although she had always been overly generous with her presents. But not this one. This one had been down to Giles.

'Your gaiety is slipping,' Jean-Marc reproved softly from beside her, and she turned, smiled, proferred her cup for more coffee. 'Sorry.' And when the other guests began to arrive, she perked up, laughed with them when they laughed at her appearance, pretended to be extrovert and happy, until Marguerite sauntered in, eyed her with dislike, or derision, or maybe both, and rudely snapped her fingers for champagne.

When breakfast was announced, they all trooped into the dining-car like excited children, Francine thought. Laughing, chattering, then exclaiming in delight at the many gift-wrapped boxes tumbled on each table. Including her own. Puzzled, she looked up as Giles came to sit opposite her.

'I may not like you,' he said quietly, 'but I would not be intentionally cruel.' Indicating the gifts, he explained, 'Something for you to open.' Which she wouldn't have had... Feeling suddenly choked, desperately sniffing, because if she grizzled, her false eyelashes were likely to fall off, she kept her head lowered, fiddled with a pink ribbon on one of the packages. 'Nothing very much, I'm afraid, because I did not expect you to turn up.'

'Why?' she asked huskily. 'I did not know I hadn't been invited. Didn't know it was a private party.'

'So I gather, but that wasn't the reason. I expected you to have better things to do.'

'Better than an exclusive train journey through Switzerland?'

'Yes.'

'And if you had thought I *would* come, would you have bought me presents?'

'Of course.'

'But you don't like me, and you don't like shopping.'

'I didn't do any. My secretary did,' he explained in answer to her silent query. 'I merely wrote a list.'

'And judging by the exquisite trappings, had them professionally wrapped,' she guessed.

'Of course.'

'Then how . . .'

With a sudden smile, he leaned conspiratorially towards her and whispered, 'I removed a few labels.'

'From presents meant for the other ladies? Things that would be suitable for any lady, regardless of age or inclination?'

'Mm.'

Staring at him for a moment in silence, her face still a little bewildered, she said quietly, 'I don't understand you.'

'Don't you?'

Helplessly indicating the presents, she murmured, 'It was a nice gesture. Thank you.'

'You're welcome. And you're supposed to open them, not admire the pretty packaging. I'll see you later.' Getting to his feet, he walked back towards the lounge.

Didn't he ever eat, she wondered? Didn't he have any presents of his own?

'Hey, Red!' someone called down the carriage, and she glanced up, smiled wryly at her friend with the twinkling blue eyes. 'Don't sit by yourself!'

'I'm OK,' she called back, 'truly.'

'Nonsense!'

Easing free of the seat, he came down to her, gathered up her packages, and began to walk back towards his own table.

Without very much choice in the matter, she picked up her bag and followed. The American couple were sitting at the table opposite, and she smiled at them and wished them happy Christmas. They smiled back, showed her their presents, and she finally undid her own. A black,

sexy negligée, which she hastily pushed back into its
wrapping when she caught her companion's amused appreciation. A scarf pin, a scarf—Hermés, she noted in
horror. Perfume, bath oil, and a box of hand-made Swiss
chocolates. And he called this not very much? Glancing
round, seeing that the others had much of the same, the
men ties, cigars, tie-pins, she shook her head in bewilderment. It must have cost him an absolute fortune. But
then he had a fortune, he'd said so.

'Do we flirt *all* the time,' her new friend enquired
teasingly, 'or only between meals?'

Startled, glancing up, she grinned. He looked so de-
lightfully *hopeful*. 'Between.'

'*D'accord*. And only in front of Giles?' he pondered
softly.

'No!' Aware that she was blushing, she looked quickly
down, then chuckled. 'But it would be *best* in front of
Giles.'

'Because?'

She shook her head and he gave a slow smile, the
twinkle even more pronounced. 'Then as Giles is not here
at the moment, we will converse naturally, yes?'

'Yes, please.' And as they ate, they chatted inconsequentially, and Francine stared out at Alpine slopes,
could make out magnificent mansions and weathered
wood chalets as they hurried past.

'Coming in to Lausanne,' he explained. 'See the Savoy
Alps on the horizon? And look,' he pointed, 'you can
just make out the tower of the cathedral.'

Nodding to show she'd seen, and that the town seemed
to be built on different levels, old and beautiful, she
glanced the other way, stared at the lake. Pewter grey,
reflecting the cloud cover, cold, and she thought she
would like to see it in summer, with a clear blue sky, with

the steamers busily plying back and forth. And everywhere looked so clean, even on such a grey day.

She continued to watch for a little while, interested in everything she saw, the busy station as they moved slowly through, a giant Christmas tree sparkling with lights and decorations. High-speed trains ran from Paris, she knew, taking a little over three hours. Much faster than their own detouring progress. But then that was the whole point of the trip. To see as much as could be seen of the magnificent countryside. When they'd finished eating, Lausanne sliding slowly behind them, they returned to the lounge. Her new name, Red, seemed very firmly on everyone's lips, she thought in amusement, except for Marguerite, who was obviously ignoring her. She was with a tall, thin man Francine hadn't seen before. He had an expression of fright on his gaunt face, and she wondered who he was.

'Her husband,' Giles said drily from behind her. 'He's been keeping to his cabin. Didn't feel very well.'

'I'm not surprised ...'

'Uh, uh,' he admonished softly.

'I was only going to say ...'

'I know what you were only going to say. Look at the scenery.'

Feeling suddenly stifled by his proximity, she gave him a distracted smile and slid into a nearby seat, a mistake, because Giles slid in beside her. Too close. Much, much too close.

'Marguerite is Claire's sister.'

Astonished that he should explain, momentarily diverted from the claustrophobia his nearness brought, she turned her head, found herself almost nose to nose with him, and jerked round to stare blindly from the window. 'Oh.'

'Quite.'

Desperately fighting to find something to say to defuse the tension that probably only she felt, she suddenly registered what she was seeing. 'Oh, how lovely!' she exclaimed.

'Montreux,' he informed her even more drily.

'It seems to spill down the hillsides...and look at those railways! Almost perpendicular!' Stop babbling, Francine.

'Oberland Bahn.' Lightly tapping her shoulder, he directed her attention across to the other side, and her eyes widened in delight. 'Château de Chillon.'

'It looks as though it's rearing out of the water!'

'Mm...'

'Giles?'

Glancing up, he smiled at someone farther down. 'Excuse me.' Faint amusement lurking in his eyes, he slid free and walked away, presumably to explain something someone had seen from the window. Watching him, admiring his strong frame, she blinked when her view was blocked, then smiled at her flirtatious friend.

'Now?' he asked wickedly.

With a helpless laugh, she reached out her hand, and knowing the gesture wouldn't be misinterpreted, gently touched her fingers to his cheek—and found Giles watching her. Snapping her eyes away, she withdrew her hand. This awareness of him was absurd! Laughable! And she didn't *care* what he thought. 'Certainly now,' she agreed, and he slid in opposite her, began to flirt outrageously—but in the nicest possible way.

As the train curved away, she lost sight of the fairy-tale castle, and looked back to the snow-covered mountains, yet was still aware of Giles at the other end of the carriage, could still almost feel his touch against her shoulder, his breath feathering her cheek. Bought and paid for. Stop it. *Stop* it!

Mountains, slopes, snowy fields, pretty villages barely touched by modern technology. Remote, wild, beautiful, and as the train ran through one spectacular view after another, she ran out of superlatives. People sat and talked quietly, watched the views, exchanged backgrounds, and gradually, the sky cleared, became a bright cerulean blue. Everything looked crisp and cold, dark shadows, bright hillsides, fir trees giving a splash of green, the brief glimpse of a cable-car swinging high above them, sun glinting off its windows.

They stopped briefly in Brig, for what reason she didn't know. Supplies maybe, and those that had thick coats and boots stretched their legs, stared at the three gilt onion domes of the Stockalperschloss, the massive baroque castle, recently restored, and she wanted to walk into the town, explore, feel the crisp snow crunch underfoot. Meet new people. Walk away from Giles—and the way he made her feel. Last to climb back aboard, she tidied herself in her cabin, replaced her boots with her shoes, and with the scent of roast turkey in her nostrils, she made her way to the dining-car.

The kitchen staff, the stewards, had all done a magnificent job, and finding that the fresh air had given her an appetite, Francine went eagerly to her table, and found that Giles was intending to lunch with her.

'I was beginning to think you didn't eat,' she said stupidly, and he raised one eyebrow, gave her a mocking look. Glancing from the window, anything really to avoid looking at him, she stared at a perpendicular track and wondered at the courage, or madness, in going in a train that ran up to heaven. A picture postcard country—and people that were unexciting, according to Giles. Perhaps it was a national joke—and meant the opposite.

'Not all banks and cuckoo clocks?' he asked with a smile.

'No, all mountains and cable-cars,' she joked back, and knew that he watched her.

Why, she wondered almost despairingly, did he have this extraordinary effect on her? Made her sharp, or tongue-tied? Unable to behave normally? Long for something undefined?

The meal was a slow, humourous affair, and Francine was grateful when people came to briefly sit at their table between courses, chat with her and Giles, joke with him, tease him. Why did they tease him? Was his behaviour such a departure from the norm? Did they think he only sat in his stuffy bank? And play golf, she remembered. And ski. And all the while, he watched her, made her uncomfortable. And when the meal was finished, brandies or liqueurs nursed in palms, she had to ask.

'Why do they tease you?'

Leaning back, totally relaxed, he smiled. 'Because they know I loathe entertaining. Because I rarely go to parties; because I do not join the smart set at St. Moritz or Klosters or wherever the current in place is; because they do not believe I am really doing this.'

'You don't like people?'

'Certainly I like people—in small doses.'

'You like to observe, don't you? Not mix.'

'Mm. And you're a mixer, aren't you, Red? A butterfly. And you don't care about people at all.'

'I care about a great many people,' she argued quietly, 'and you shouldn't jump to conclusions on a few ill-chosen words Mally might have said.'

'Where you're concerned, jumping to conclusions is probably a safe bet.'

'Is it?' Feeling hurt, she began to gather her things together. 'Excuse me. I really don't think I want to listen to this. And just because you paid for me doesn't give you the right to insult me.'

'My friendship with Mally gives me the right to be angry on her behalf.'

'No, it doesn't. Mally loved me, as I loved her, and we understood each other very well.'

'Yes. Sadly, she understood you only too well. And if you understood her as you thought you did, why hurt her so badly?'

'I did not hurt her!' she answered angrily. 'From the age of eight, she was my tutor, my mentor, my confidante. I knew her as well as anyone! So don't you dare rubbish my feelings for her! Or hers for me!' Jerking to her feet, face tight, she picked up her bag, and walked out towards the sleeping carriage.

He caught her up, took her arm, and brought her to a halt. Leaning her against the pannelling, he stood in front of her, his face harsh. 'She loved you and you let her down all along the line! She said—'

'I don't want to know what she said!' she broke in savagely. 'She loved me, I know she did, and I will not believe she said anything derogatory. It's *your* interpretation that's made me out to be selfish, amoral.'

Capturing her hand, he said coldly, 'Don't poke me in the chest.'

'You'd prefer I poke you in the eye? Because, believe me, the way I feel right now, I'd decapitate you if I could!' She very rarely lost her temper, was very rarely hurt enough or goaded enough, but she was hurt now, her feelings still raw from a death that had taken her by surprise, shocked her, and she wasn't *ready* to talk about her yet, discuss her feelings. 'And what gives you the God-given right to treat me as though you're the keeper of my soul?'

'Mally does.'

'Don't call her that! That's *my* name for her!'

Turning her head aside, she stared blindly down the corridor.

'You're crying,' he said softly.

'So?' she demanded defiantly.

'Why would Mally tell me things about you if they weren't true?'

'I don't know. I don't know why she should tell you *anything!* I'd never even *heard* of you! And if you were the great friends you insist, I *would* have done!'

'Not necessarily. Mally kept her personal life separate from her business affairs.'

'Meaning her money.' With an inelegant snort that hopefully disguised her distress, she said flatly, 'And I suppose now you're going to accuse me of only wanting her wealth!'

'No, because at the end of the day there was very little to leave, as I'm sure you're well aware.'

'Yes,' she gritted. 'So how long *had* you known her?'

'Years. My father used to administer the estate when her husband was alive, and after my father's retirement, her husband's death, I inherited her affairs. I used to fly in to see her two or three times a year. I was very fond of her.'

'And I *loved* her!'

His face thoughtful, he continued to stare down at her. 'Why didn't you go to the funeral?'

'Because I had flu,' she said baldly.

'I see.'

'Good.' Shoving past him, she hurried into her compartment, slammed the door shut. Dragging a deep, distraught breath into her lungs, she slowly released it, stared miserably ahead. She hadn't deserved that. She *knew* she hadn't. So what she would do was, when they left the train at Bad Ragaz, went to the hotel, she would make alternative arrangements to get home. She could probably get a train to Zurich, fly home from there. She would remove all this garish make-up, tidy herself, and go back to the lounge, sit and talk quietly with people, and in a few hours they would be at the hotel, and everything would be all right.

Straightening, she picked up her make-up bag and began to put herself to rights. Removing the silly flower, she brushed her hair, sprayed on some perfume, took a deep breath, and walked out. Giles was waiting outside, leaning back against the window bar opposite, and after one brief look, turned resolutely away, only to be halted.

'I didn't mean to upset you,' he said quietly. 'Didn't know I *could*.'

'You didn't upset me,' she denied quickly. 'But you surely couldn't think your insults would make me *laugh!*'

'No.' His expression pensive, he finally murmured, 'Marie Louise was old, old-fashioned maybe, and didn't understand modern ways, perhaps, interpreted your behaviour wrongly.'

'Perhaps,' she agreed coldly, her face still averted.

'And I somehow didn't expect it to matter to you what I thought.'

'It doesn't!'

He gave an odd smile, turned her to face him. 'You've lost your flower.'

'I took it off,' she said shortly.

'Not allowed.' Reaching behind her, he broke off another one, tucked it carefully behind her ear, and the feel of his long fingers on her neck, her hair, made her shiver, try to pull away.

'What's wrong? Cold?'

'No.' How could she be cold? The heating on the train was more than adequate. 'Let me go, Giles, I really don't think there's anything more to say.'

Ignoring her, his thumbs on her jaw, he gently forced her face up. 'I don't understand you—and I couldn't believe Mally lied. And yet, even if all she said is true, even knowing what I do about you, I still want to touch you. Kiss you. But then, you know that, don't you? Have known it since I kissed you last night.'

'No,' she denied woodenly, but that awful flutter had started again inside, and she resolutely kept her eyes down.

'Don't lie.'

Glaring at him, she demanded, 'Why *did* you kiss me? Derision? Punishment?'

'No,' he denied simply. 'Because I wanted to.'

'And that makes it all right?'

'No.' Thumbs still on her jaw, he slid his fingers beneath her hair, lowered his head to hers, just barely touched her mouth with his—and she jerked as though she'd been bitten.

'Don't,' she muttered thickly.

'Then fight me off.'

'No.' She groaned in shock, and felt as helpless as a rag doll when he tilted her face towards his, touched his mouth once more to hers. A gentle, unbelievably erotic exploration, and she groaned again, deep inside, felt her body melt, and deliberately forced herself away. Breathing ragged, she glared at him, but when his palms slid to her back, eased her closer, she let him, actually *let* him, melted into an embrace as though she had no will-power of her own, which at the moment, she didn't. Only part of her mind insisted she struggle free, the rest gave in to pleasure. Unbelievably shaming, but she *wanted* this! And it was only what he would expect, wasn't it? If he thought her a tramp?

Sliding her hands to his chest, she let them rest there, and feeling dazed and unreal, she looked into his eyes. Eyes that were no longer angry or sombre, or indifferent. Eyes that searched hers before moving to her mouth, and then he was kissing her again, gently, touch and release, touch, taste, and desire that had been building since the very first time she saw him spiralled into longing, and so she kissed him back. The one spark he'd been waiting for as she was crushed into an embrace where urgency and passion were no longer muted.

To feel, to be touched, to kiss and be kissed, was all that mattered. The scent of him, the warm, strong feel of him, the pleasure and the pain, and the thunder of the train on the track matched the thunder of her heart. They kissed with hunger, seemingly with mutual need, and her body roused as if from a long sleep as she stretched against him, fit herself more comfortably to his large frame, felt his strength, his control, his desire.

'I *knew* I wasn't wrong,' he breathed softly.

'Wrong?'

'Mm. My cabin's at the end,' he added thickly as his mouth moved to her cheek, her ear, and back again.

'What?'

'My cabin. Be more comfortable.'

Suddenly aware of where this was leading, suddenly frightened, she shook her head.

'Yes.'

'No,' she whispered, and he drew back, stared at her.

'No?' he demanded softly.

'No.'

'Why?'

'Because I don't know you, because . . .'

'It's never stopped you before.'

Stilling, she stared at him. 'What?'

'I said, it's never stopped you before. You give to everyone else, why not me?'

'Is *that* what this is all about?' she demanded in disbelief. 'To prove a *point?*' Without even thinking about it, considering it, she shoved him away, drew back her hand and tried to slap his arrogant face. He caught her wrist easily, as though he might have had plenty of practice, increased the pressure of his fingers until pain began to cramp her arm—and there was a rumble, like thunder. Stiffening, he tilted his head as though the better to listen, and still holding her by the wrist, grabbed the window bar just as the train jerked, followed by high-pitched squealing as the brakes were urgently applied. The abrupt deceleration caused the carriage to sway alarmingly, force them backwards, then rock violently as the driver fought to halt the fast-running train.

'Grab hold of something!' Giles shouted urgently. But the only thing to grab hold of was him.

Chapter Three

AND then the train slammed to a violent halt and they were thrown forward. Giles's grip on the bar prevented them falling, but momentum dragged Francine round to slam painfully into the side of the carriage. She grunted, froze, waited for what else might come, and then Giles moved, breaking the stasis.

'Make sure everyone's all right,' he ordered quickly, 'I need to see what's happened.'

She nodded dazedly as he flung open the outside door, letting in a cold blast of air, jumped down, then slammed it behind him. Pulling herself together, she hurried into the shambles of the lounge. Everyone had obviously frozen, as she had, clutched whatever, or whoever, was nearest, and then all been toppled like cards along with anything else that hadn't been bolted down. Plates, glasses, bottles, bowls of savouries. And the silence was deafening—until Marguerite began to scream.

'Shut up,' someone snapped. Surprisingly, she did.

Hurrying toward a woman who was lying on the floor, her husband crouched over her, Francine checked her swiftly with her eyes, knelt, whispered, 'All right? Can you move?'

She nodded, and they helped her up and into a seat. Nervous conversation started up, shaken laughter, as people began to sort themselves out. Grabbing a serviette, Francine hastened down the carriage, handed it to a man who had blood trickling down his forehead, then looked hastily round for any other injuries, checked that everyone was accounted for.

'Giles?' someone queried.

'Gone to find out what happened,' she answered quickly with an automatic smile of reassurance, and then the train groaned, as though under unbelievable pressure, and a collective breath was held, then released, a soft susurrating sigh. Her smile just a bit shaky, she turned her head, and blinked in astonishment. All the windows on the left were white. She could almost see individual crystals as the mass pressed against the windows. An avalanche? There was a groan from behind her, and she whirled round, saw Jean-Marc stagger to his feet behind the bar. He was cradling one arm to his chest and blood was dripping sluggishly from his hand onto the bar top.

Hurriedly picking her way across to him through the debris that crunched and snapped underfoot, wrinkling her nose at the overpowering smell of spirits from smashed bottles, she snatched up a napkin from the floor and eased his arm free. It was difficult to see for all the blood, but it looked like his palm. Sweeping the debris off the bar with her forearm, she hitched up her skirt, clambered over, and forced him to hold his hand under the cold tap. A deep ragged cut ran diagonally across his palm. Shaking out the napkin to make sure there was no glass in it, she folded it into a square. Drawing his hand from under the water, she pressed the pad to it. 'Press hard,' she instructed him.

Still looking dazed, he nodded, and she looked round for something to secure it with, then smiled her thanks when someone offered his tie.

'Bad?' he asked.

'Needs stitching, and he needs to sit down.'

As they helped him out, she saw Giles. He was standing just inside the doorway, watching her. She raised an eyebrow, and he shook his head, glanced quickly round as though to assess damage, then disappeared again. She hadn't forgotten his behaviour, but now was not the time to be difficult; ignore him, as she wished. Hate him, as she wished.

Seating Jean-Marc with an older woman who looked very shaken, gently instructing her to keep an eye on him, mostly because it would give her something to do, take her mind off herself, she told the steward to keep his hand up.

'Avalanche?' he asked quietly.

'Looks like it.'

He nodded. 'Giles will know what to do.' Obviously making a great effort, he smiled, tried to make a little joke. 'Very efficient, the Swiss. I expect they 'ave radioed ahead and within a short while we will be on our way again.'

'Yes.' They looked at each other, smiled, tried to look as though they both believed it.

'And you make the very efficient doctor,' he praised.

'I took an extensive first aid course,' she explained absently. When Mally had been ill, and she hadn't known what to do.

'Red?'

Turning, she walked down to where her grey-haired companion was beckoning. He nodded to the Frenchwoman sitting at the rear. Angelique, Francine thought her name was. Married to Claude.

'I think she's broken her arm,' he whispered.

Nodding, Francine went to have a look, smiled reassuringly, tested it gently, and comforted, 'Only bruised,

I think, but I'll strap it across you just in case.' Removing her scarf, she fashioned a sling and gently applied it.

Everyone still looked a bit shaken, but beginning to recover. Most of the men were heading for the doorway where Giles had appeared to see for themselves what had happened, and Francine, being no less curious than anyone else, but not wanting to see Giles, headed in the opposite direction. She needed to find the kitchens, anyway. Yet as she reached the connecting doorway, she suddenly wondered why she didn't feel shocked or frightened. Because she didn't, she realised, she felt abnormally calm. Or maybe she was still too shaken from the earlier disaster to feel very much for this one. The disaster of his kiss, because it was a disaster, and now that the immediate danger seemed to be over, she couldn't get it out of her head, or the taste from her mouth. Or his subsequent behaviour from her mind. She wanted to go somewhere quiet to think about it, rationalise it. Dismiss it. She had been kissed a great many times in her twenty-eight years, but never like that. Never had there been so much *feeling*. Such a rush of—*need*. And she wanted to feel it again, wanted total immersion, but not with him. Never with him, she assured herself grimly. Her mouth tight, eyes bleak, she hurried through the diningroom, the dining-room that now looked as though a bomb had hit it. Cups, glasses, bottles, cloths had slid from the tables, lay scattered on benches and floor. With a little sigh, she hurried on, and before going into what were presumably the kitchens, she eased open the outer door and peered out.

It looked cold and cheerless, the sky beginning to grow dark, soft fat flakes of snow drifting down, as though innocent of all harm, but she couldn't see what had caused the train to halt. The snow beside the track had been tramped down, all the toing and froing of the engineer, the guard, Giles, maybe, and curiosity getting the better of common sense, she climbed carefully down, shivered in the cold air, and inched along to the front of the train, then gasped. A mound of unbroken white as far as the eye could see, the track completely buried. Taking a step back, she stared up at the train, saw the overhang of white from the roof.

'What are you doing?' Giles demanded angrily from behind her. 'It is not a game! A spectacle for sightseeing!'

Swinging round, she saw him standing with another man, the driver perhaps, both almost knee deep in snow. The driver had his arms hugged round himself for warmth. Giles looked as though cold never touched him.

'Get back inside at once. You'll freeze to death in that skimpy frock.'

'It isn't skimpy,' she denied dismissively. 'And I didn't for one moment assume it was a game!' Praying she wouldn't do anything stupid, like fall over, she hurried back to the doorway, looked briefly up at the mountains before climbing inside. If that lot came down, as well . . .

Shivering, forcing the thought aside, she reached for the handle of the door to the kitchen just as Giles swung himself into the carriage behind her. He stamped his feet to get rid of the excess snow, closed the door behind him, trapping her with him between the inner and outer doors. He made no immediate move to enter the dining-car, just stared down at her.

'That was a damned silly thing to have done.'

'Was it?' she asked coldly. 'At least I wasn't standing knee deep in snow.' Relieved to find that her voice sounded ordinary, cool, she added, 'How bad is it?'

'Bad enough. The engineer is awaiting instructions. We need to know how much snow is above us, whether moving will bring the lot down. A relief train is on its way.'

'Ah, yes, the efficient Swiss, who are so very unexciting.' Angry with him, with herself, and beginning to feel stifled, she turned away, reached for the inner door, and he halted her, put a hand on her shoulder.

'Red...'

Breathing suspended, she gritted, 'Don't touch me.'

Removing his hand, his tone hardened, and he obviously changed what he'd been going to say. 'Don't go spreading alarm and despondency,' he ordered. 'I want no hysteria.'

'I never get hysterical,' she refuted equally coldly. 'Neither do I spread alarm and despondency.'

'No,' he agreed, and for a moment sounded almost weary. 'Only dejection.' Without waiting for her to comment further, he pushed past her and into the dining-car.

Dejection? The only person she'd dejected was herself. Her sigh bitter, she walked into the kitchen, sympathised with them at the mess, enquired about injuries, then asked if hot drinks were possible. Five minutes, she was told, and when she returned to the lounge it was to find that people had been busy. The debris had all been swept up, optics replaced, and although it wasn't quite a party atmosphere, everyone seemed more or less cheerful. Going to check on Jean-Marc, keeping her eyes very firmly away from Giles, she sat, checked his wound, and stayed where she was. And when tea had been served, fidgeting had begun, the little wall telephone buzzed, and Giles answered it—and everyone stopped talking, turned to face him, and like obedient sheep, waited for the oracle to speak, she thought bitterly.

He listened for a few minutes, then replaced the handset. 'The relief train will be here in about half an hour. I'm afraid it will mean getting cold and wet as we'll have to walk past the blockage to reach it, so dress warmly. Anything you need for the hotel put in a case, bag, whatever, and leave it outside your cabin door. The stewards will bring them. This train, hopefully, will be ready and waiting for us tomorrow morning. I'm sorry for the temporary disruption to our plans.' He nodded his thanks, went across to have a brief word with Jean-Marc, then Angelique, and Francine walked quietly back to her cabin to pack.

The ladies without boots were carried by Giles, Marguerite being one of them. Francine had boots, thankfully, and brought up the rear with the American couple.

Brightly shone the moon that night, though the frost was cruel... Irritated with herself, and wishing she didn't have to follow in anyone's footsteps, let alone those of Good King Wenceslas, she quickened her pace. The sooner she was on the other train, the sooner they'd be in Chur. It took them a while to negotiate the five hundred yards or so, and although it was cold, the night was utterly still, silent, no ominous rumbling from overhead.

Marguerite deposited, Giles came back to make sure they were all right. Or make sure the American woman was. She couldn't imagine he cared about her, not after the things he'd said. Taking the American woman from them, he swung her up into his arms and walked off. 'Don't dawdle,' he called over his shoulder.

Her companion looked a little startled, but Francine didn't bother to explain that it had been directed at her, not him. Clambering thankfully into the relief train, into warmth, they divested themselves of their outer clothing, and took their seats, and within minutes were on their way to Chur.

Once past Munster, they picked up speed, slowed for the Furka Pass, the long tunnel that linked Oberwald and Realp, and although she was nervous of tunnels, her mind was more concerned with making tentative plans, of reaching the hotel, of leaving, getting back home. And never seeing Giles again. Giles, who was currently having a brief word with everyone. The perfect host. When he reached their seats, she stared from the window, ignored him, was aware of him chatting easily to the couple opposite, something about the dollar against the Swiss franc, then on to a discussion about people she didn't know. No longer listening, she started when he nudged her, queried smoothly, 'Isn't that right, Red?'

'Pardon?'

'So aloof?' he queried. His eyes mocking her, he repeated, 'I was just explaining why you were ignoring me.'

Eyes widening in alarm, then fury, that he should actually discuss what had taken place between them, she glared at him, then frowned in confusion when he added blandly, 'It was a very silly thing to do without a coat on.'

'What?' Realising he was playing with her, like a cat with a mouse, she gave him a sugary smile. 'Not silly when you do it, because *you* were gleaning important information, of course.'

'Certainly.'

'But when a woman does it, it's called being nosy or silly. Although you are right,' she added, her smile sweeter, 'I should never have gone out without a coat. I might have caught my death.'

'Thereby negating the need to tell you off,' he agreed smoothly.

Sorely tempted to take the wind out of his sails, tell them the truth, that the reason she was ignoring him was because he'd kissed her and then insulted her, she opened her mouth, stared into his eyes, eyes dancing with wicked derision, and shut it again with a snap. Thought it funny, did he? That she'd tried to slap him? And that didn't make very much sense. Most men, she assumed, would have been furious. Hurt pride alone would have dictated that, wouldn't it? But perhaps he was furious, just managed to hide it better.

'Don't worry about it,' he soothed with about as much sincerity as a rat.

'I wasn't,' she denied. 'Don't let us keep you. I'm sure you're eager to talk to your other guests.'

He nodded blandly and thankfully left, and she heard him say something to the people behind her. Aware that the Americans were watching her oddly, she forced herself to smile.

'Not long now,' she murmured inanely, and when they eventually pulled into Chur station, she could hear a clock striking somewhere, and automatically counted the strokes. Seven, and in a few more hours, with luck, she could be on her way. *If* the scheduled trains ran on Christmas Day. If not, first thing in the morning.

Standing, ready to leave, Giles halted them for a moment. 'If you could all assemble in the station forecourt it will be easier to organise you into the transport arranged to take you to the hotel. My apologies once again for the delay.' He gave his economical smile, and stepped down from the train. And as Francine did the same, the first person she saw was Claire. The woman from Paris. And even if she hadn't recognised her, Marguerite's loud exclamation would have told her. She was standing by the exit like an extra from *Doctor Zhivago*. Long fur coat, matching fur hat, boots. Posed. Don't be bitchy, Francine. Feeling extraordinarily weary, she glanced to where Giles was standing, courteously ensuring that everyone got off safely. He, too, was watching Claire, but his face gave nothing away of how he was feeling. Or had he expected her to be here?

As she walked along the platform, she watched Marguerite and Claire greet each other, and was surprised by the coolness both showed. After Marguerite's continuous demands to know where she was, she would have expected smiles, relief, warmth. Instead, they seemed not to even like each other.

'I wonder why she was so eager to find her,' Francine murmured to herself, and was astonished when the woman behind her answered.

'Because she didn't want her to have gone to Greece with some millionaire she'd found. And if she wasn't on the train, that's probably where she'd gone. Except she obviously didn't, otherwise she wouldn't be here.'

'But I thought she was involved with Giles! And Marguerite's married,' she exclaimed.

The woman raised an eyebrow. 'Don't be naïve, dear. Women like that marry for expediency. Wealth, background, social standing, and the rivalry between the sisters is—outstanding.'

Francine continued to watch, almost unable to help herself. Claire removed herself from her sister's clutching arm, and then Marguerite said something, and they both looked towards Francine. Marguerite with triumph, Claire with cool curiosity, then a dismissive smile before walking towards Giles. And she *was* beautiful. Extraordinarily so, and even though she didn't want to, Francine watched them meet. Claire reached out, put her arms round his neck, stood on tiptoe, and kissed him.

Feeling sick, she turned away. Hurrying along the platform, she stopped abruptly when Marguerite stepped into her path. With a little smirk, the other woman said softly, 'No comparison, is there?'

'Nor with you?' Not very nice, but sometimes you had to fight fire with fire. Moving round her, feeling somehow diminished by the exchange, she hurried to catch up with the other guests, and if it hadn't been for her luggage, which was being transferred separately, she would have continued on into the town, found herself another hotel. Then she suddenly remembered that she hadn't said goodbye to Jean-Marc, wished him well. Glancing round, unable to see him, she sighed. I want to go home, she thought sadly. And yet, she'd met some nice people, the Americans, the man with twinkling blue eyes. And if it hadn't been for Giles, she would have thoroughly enjoyed herself.

As promised, transport was waiting for them, horse-drawn sleighs. Gold bells cheerfully jingled when they tossed their heads, snorted in the cold air, and Francine broke into a smile of pure delight, her troubles for the moment forgotten. Walking forward, she patted the nearest horse's neck. He threw up his head, regarded her briefly, and snorted. Chuckling, she climbed in, made room for two more, settled her end of the rug warmly round her knees, and then caught Giles watching her. Tossing her head, much as the horse had done, she deliberately looked away.

Narrow streets, cobblestone alleys, ancient shuttered buildings. And a twelfth-century cathedral, where they briefly halted to listen to a choir. They were gathered outside, twenty or more, all in national dress, bright lamps cheerfully holding the dark at bay. A small band stood behind them, instruments poised, and when all the sleighs had halted, when it was silent, they began. She recognised the tune, if not the words. 'The First Noel,' and her throat tightened, a film of tears across her vision. That particular carol always did that to her, she didn't know why. Blinking rapidly, she sat entranced as the descant soared away into the still night.

Following the sound, staring upwards at the stars, so bright, so clear now that the snow had stopped, she moved her gaze to the fairy-tale forests above the town, all dusted with snow.

'Oh,' someone whispered beside her, 'how beautiful. Now it really feels like Christmas.'

Too choked to speak, Francine merely nodded, and when the sleighs moved slowly on, the choir followed all the way to the hotel—the exceptionally grand hotel—still singing. They came inside with them, were greeted warmly by the hotel staff, and given hot drinks and food. Happening to be standing near to one of the singers, Francine touched her arm, smiled, quietly thanked her, and found she still wanted to cry.

'Your key.'

Snapping round, blinking, she stared at the key held out, then up to Giles's face. He looked stern.

'Thank you,' she said quietly as she removed it from his palm.

'Your case will be delivered to your room in a few minutes.'

Nodding, she turned away, and spotting the lifts, hurried towards them. Her room could only be described as sumptuous. No expense spared, even for an interloper. Her case sat tidily at the foot of the bed, and on the dressing table was a note from the management. No, not a note, an invitation, gilt edged. Cinderella *will* go to the ball. And even if she wasn't Cinderella, there was a ball.

A fancy dress one. At the stroke of nine. And in brackets, hand written, it said, Costume in wardrobe.

Curious, she went to look. White, long, vaguely Grecian, and extraordinarily revealing. A small bag containing needle and cotton was pinned carefully at the waist, and, tucked at the bottom, a pair of gold, strappy sandals, and a strip of tiny white flowers, presumably for her hair. Dumbstruck, she continued to stare at them for some moments in silence. By whose choice, she wondered? An impersonal management? Or Giles? But Giles hadn't known she was coming, had he? Not that it made much difference, because she wasn't going. Closing the wardrobe door, she went to unlatch her case. A shower, something to eat, then she would find out about trains. So why did that feel like cheating Mally? Have a good time. Promise me, she had said. And Francine had. The last thing Mally had asked of her.

If it hadn't been for Giles… Oh, to hell with Giles, she thought in sudden anger. For twenty-four hours she'd weakly allowed herself to be insulted, kissed, propositioned … Well, no more. She *would* go to the ball! She'd flirt with every man she met, married or no. It was Christmas, and she was sick to death of allowing him to dictate the rules! She would leave in the morning.

Five to nine. Staring rather dubiously at herself in the long mirror, she wavered. Her hair looked OK, she thought. With the help of the ribbon she'd managed to twist it into a vague semblance of something Grecian. It was the dress that was causing her problems. Despite the needlework she had done, it still *revealed!* Not only one thigh, because the skirt was split almost to the hip, but the whole of one shoulder, and came dangerously near to exposing one breast. Because of the cut she couldn't wear a bra.... Hearing a bark of laughter from the corridor, muffled giggles, she eased open her door, peeped out at several costumed guests making their way down the corridor, then gave a startled blink at what looked to be an entire ostrich hovering at head height, the cause of all the merriment. Peering under the overhang, she recognised her grey-haired companion and bit her lip.

'Do not laugh,' he warned.

'But what are you supposed to *be*?'

'A Musketeer, I think.'

'But Musketeers didn't wear ostriches on their heads!'

'How do you know? And at least I am not *déshabille!*'

'Yes, well . . . I think I'd just about decided not to go.'

He grunted, walked across, leaned inside her room, grabbed her bag and key, pulled her into the corridor, and slammed her door shut. 'It's too late now.'

They stared at each other, giggled. 'Oh, what the heck. It is Christmas.'

'Oui.'

'Be brave soldiers?'

'Oui.'

Arm in arm, laughing helplessly as they took baby steps to avoid exposing Francine's leg for all and sundry to see, not to mention the two pairs of knickers she'd put on just to be on the safe side, they descended the grand staircase behind the others, and went to the ball. Then blinked. Tented in white silk, porticoed, pillared, peopled with ancient Romans, ancient Britons, Vikings, Japanese warlords, geishas, what looked like the entire charge of the Light Brigade; pirates, noblemen, women of doubtful virtue, and a large lady who looked like a cross between Queen Elizabeth I and Miss Marple, Francine made a funny little sound in the back of her throat.

Prismed light was positively flung from the enormous chandelier, bounced off the ornate decorations on the gigantic Christmas tree that stood in one corner, glittered on the brass section of the full orchestra, and gloriously highlighted the garlanded folly, complete with Greek urn, which held the buffet.

'Oh, I *am* glad we came!' Francine exclaimed in delight.

'*Oui,*' he agreed helplessly.

'I don't think I have ever *seen* anything so splendid.'

'*Non.*' Amongst all the strangers, hotel guests presumably, she could pick out several of their own party. Marguerite, trust Marguerite, *was* dressed as Cinderella. The *after* variety, and obviously looking for her Prince. Giles, presumably—in which she did him an injustice, because he hadn't bothered to dress up at all. Well, he had, but not in costume. He wore his dinner suit. Perhaps he thought dressing up was for children. She didn't see Claire. He caught her eyes, and she deliberately turned her head away, smiled at her companion. 'Something to eat?' she asked casually.

After eating, drinking several glasses of punch which gave her a rather nice glow, and judging by the way everyone was behaving, most definitely released inhibitions, Francine decided, quite forcefully, to enjoy herself. Someone had stolen her flirtatious friend, but there were plenty of other men eager and willing to dance with her, and so long as she remembered to keep her left arm clamped to her side and take small steps, all would be well. She was aware from time to time of Giles watching her, and once, when she was flirting outrageously with the King of Siam, he actually came up to her, his face set, and whilst the king turned to answer someone, Giles drew her rather forcefully to one side.

'Stop making a spectacle of yourself.'

'Why? It's what you expected, isn't it? And you chose the dress.'

'I did not.'

'Ah. You'd have put me in armour?'

'Hey,' the king exclaimed as he realised someone was trying to cut in. 'Find your own partner.'

She didn't understand Giles's reply. Probably said in Swiss, but judging by his expression, it had been something pithy and to the point. Not that she cared.

'No Claire?' she asked sweetly.

'No,' he denied stonily.

'So sad.' With a sugary smile, and showing rather a lot of leg, she whirled away with her king.

'What's his problem?' the king asked.

'I've no idea,' she denied. And she didn't, not really. She hadn't been flirting with any of *his* friends. Anyway, she had no ties, no boyfriend, husband, and she hadn't upset anyone's wife, only flirted with those who flirted with her, but every time she caught sight of Giles's reproving face, even though she told herself she didn't care, it goaded her to behave even more outrageously— well, maybe not outrageously, but certainly not how she usually behaved. Of course, the punch might have had something to do with it. Not that she was drunk, just— exhilarated. Or had been. His scathing comments had rather spoilt the mood.

Dancing with a nice woodsman, beginning to feel hot and somewhat dishevelled, she excused herself, made her way towards the powder room.

'Francine?'

Turning, seeing the American woman, dressed rather incongruously as Medusa, moving towards her, she waited—and then saw who else was heading her way.

'Francine?' Giles queried somewhat accusingly.

Giving him a brief look of dislike, she turned away.

'She called you Francine.'

'So?'

'Why?' he demanded.

'Why what?' she asked irritably as she took another step away.

He grabbed her arm. 'Why,' he asked with heavy patience, 'are you calling yourself Francine?'

'I'm not *calling* myself anything! And take your hand off my arm! Hello, Medusa, did you want me?'

'Only to say good-night dear.' Smiling at her, she leaned forward to kiss her cheek. 'I'm pooped. I'll see you in the morning.' Turning to Giles, she reached up to kiss him also, patted his shoulder, and added with smiling reproval, 'Stop scowling at poor Francine. People will begin to think you don't like her.'

'He doesn't,' Francine growled pithily, and she laughed, disbelieving.

'That's a sock that won't wash. It's perfectly obvious how you feel about each other.' With a suggestive little grin, she whispered, 'Good night. I won't tell you to behave.' Leaving a grim-faced Giles to face an equally grim-faced Francine, he grabbed her arm, hauled her to one side, out of view of the rest of the guests, and repeated angrily, 'Why?'

'Presumably,' she enunciated icily, 'because that's my name. What did you think it was, Desdemona?'

'No,' he denied in quiet fury. 'Cecille.'

Chapter Four

'CECILLE?' she exclaimed in astonishment. 'Don't be so insulting! I'm nothing like Cecille! And I utterly resent you implying that I am!'

There was a long, long silence as the anger in his eyes turned slowly to perplexity. 'Aren't?'

'What?' Staring at him, her own fury giving way to bewilderment, she queried slowly, 'Are you saying that you *really* thought I was Cecille?'

'Well, of course I thought you were Cecille! Who else was I supposed to think you were? Are you telling me you aren't?'

'Well, doesn't that just take the biscuit! You thought I was *Cecille?* Cecille who is...who... How dare you! She's the most amoral little alley cat it's ever been my misfortune to meet—' Breaking off, she stared at him in shock. '*That's* why you...'

'Yes,' he agreed quietly.

Searching his face, her mouth suddenly tightened. 'The last I heard,' she bit out, 'Cecille was in Florida. So if you want a bed mate, I suggest you go and find her!'

'I do not want a bed mate! And certainly not Cecille.'

'Don't lie! Thinking I was Cecille, you tried to get me into your cabin!'

'Thinking you were Cecille,' he shot back, 'I *expected* you to go to my cabin!'

'Which is exactly the same thing!'

'No, it is not! Expecting and wanting are two entirely different things!'

'But they would have had the same ending, wouldn't they? If I had gone. Humiliation.'

With a little shrug, he continued, 'So, if you aren't Cecille, who are you?'

Furious, she gave him a nasty little smile. 'Well,' she drawled insultingly, 'I was on the station, and I saw this wonderful little train, and I thought...'

Gripping her arm, halting not only her pat little speech but her blood flow, he ground out, 'Why are you here?'

'Because Mally *invited* me!' she answered.

'Mally invited Cecille! She wrote and told me, remember?'

'Mally hadn't seen Cecille in over a year! She didn't even *like* her, so she would hardly have invited her to come on your wretched train!'

'She *wrote*,' he snarled.

'I don't care what she did! She wouldn't have invited *Cecille!*' Wrenching herself free of him with a savage movement that nearly sent him off balance, she stormed towards the powder room. He caught her arm, shoved her into the doorway next to it, which happened to be a utility room, groped around for a light switch, and yanked it on. Setting his back against the door, he folded his arms and glared at her. 'Now, the truth! Why are you here? And why are you pretending to be Cecille?'

'I was not pretending to be Cecille! Did I tell you that was my name? No, I did not! Did I tell anyone else? No! And if you *remember*,' she emphasised as she just remembered herself, 'I tried to introduce myself and you pokily informed me that you knew who I was! Aha,' she exclaimed when he suddenly frowned. '*Now* who's fault is it?'

Looking irritated and furious, he stated coldly, 'Which brings us back to why you are here.'

'Because Mally booked tickets for us both on the Europa Express for a Christmas break. Or so I thought. I did not know you had invited her. I did not know you hadn't invited me! *All* I knew was what she told me, gave me, and then, before she died, her insistence that I come. Made me promise, in fact.'

He glared at her, searched her face, demanded, 'Who *are* you?'

'Francine!'

'Francine *who?*'

'Ward!'

'I've never heard of any Francine Ward!'

'Well, that's hardly my fault, is it?'

He sighed again, ground his teeth. 'What are you, her maid?'

'Her maid?' she exclaimed in astonishment. 'No, I am not her maid! And even if I was, there's no need to damned well sneer! In fact, her maid is as good as any of the fine fancy friends you have here!'

'I didn't say she wasn't! Didn't even imply it! So what are you? Some distant relative? Companion? What?'

'Her goddaughter!'

'Her. . .' Frowning, he stared at her in astonishment, then looked disgusted. 'Don't lie!'

'I'm not lying!'

'You have to be, because you can't be her goddaughter!'

'Why can't I?' she demanded haughtily.

'Because. . .'

'Because what?' she snapped. 'Well?' she asked impatiently when he only continued to stare at her in frowning silence. 'Because what?'

'Because you're too old!'

'*Old?* I'm twenty-eight!'

'And her goddaughter is a small child! My little god-daughter, she would say, a dear child...'

'Yes, well...' she muttered in embarrassment. 'She tended to forget I'd grown up. And I was little, compared to her, and I suppose when you're eighty-seven, anyone under thirty *is* a child. By comparison. But be that as it may, she *did* invite me! And I *am* her god-daughter!'

Staring at her for long moments in frowning silence, he suddenly swore. '*That's* why I was surprised.'

'What?'

'You didn't seem like she'd always said you were, said Cecille was, and it confused me.'

'And that's an apology, is it?' she asked tartly.

'What? No,' he denied, his face still creased in thought. 'But you said...'

'A great many things, I expect,' she broke in smartly, 'and now if you'll kindly open the door...'

With a slow blink, he focused on her face again, absently shook his head. 'Then if you aren't her, aren't remotely like her, why did my crack about married men irk you?'

'None of your business,' she denied shortly, 'and I wish to leave.' Now that her anger and confusion were dying, she was becoming only too well aware of his proximity, and with that knowledge came the feeling of stiflement, of how very masculine he was, how very small the cupboard. And how much she disliked him.

'Goddaughter, granddaughter,' he murmured to himself, 'could be. Her writing was very shaky.'

'How magnanimous,' she derided, and giving a long sigh, filled with as much sarcasm as she could muster, she drawled haughtily, 'Could you ruminate later? I wish to leave. And I'm *sure* your guests must be wondering where you are.'

'Guests? Oh, I doubt it.' Staring at her, he suddenly smiled, a real smile, one that crinkled his eyes. 'It's good to know that my instincts haven't entirely left me.'

Fighting to remain unmoved by his smile, mentally cataloguing all the insults he'd thrown at her over the past twenty-four hours, she queried insincerely, 'Is it? How nice—now let me out.'

'Because it was very disturbing,' he continued taking not the slightest bit of notice of her request, 'to enjoy kissing a woman I thought I despised. And now, of course...'

With a disbelieving laugh, which held just the tiniest trace of fear, she exclaimed, 'You expect me to forgive and forget? Carry on as though none of it matters? Allow you to *kiss* me again just because you *enjoyed* it?'

'Of course. Because you enjoyed it, too, didn't you?' he asked softly. 'And Medusa did say...'

'I don't care what Medusa said!' she refuted in alarm as he took a step towards her. 'You touch me and...'

'And?'

'I'll scream!'

'How very unoriginal,' he drawled with another slow smile.

'I don't *feel* original!'

'No, you feel nervous.'

'No, I do not! I merely have no desire to hold this ridiculous conversation in a broom cupboard.'

'Then where shall we hold it?'

'Nowhere!' she snapped, goaded.

'Because most women,' he informed her, 'would give their right arms to hold this sort of conversation with me in a broom cupboard.'

'Well, I'm not most women. And don't be so insufferably arrogant.'

'But it's true, they've said so. Giles, they say, I would adore to have a conversation with you in a broom cupboard.'

'Shut up.'

'Because you see, I am so very wealthy. I told you that, did I not? Deliberately, of course, because I thought you were Cecille.'

'Will you stop this ridiculous nonsense and let me out!'

'No, and it is not in the least ridiculous. It helps, of course, that I do not look like the Hunchback of Notre Dame, or a troll, but I do assure you it is true. Women like me very much. Giles, they say, you are so masculine, so wonderful ... Almost, you smiled,' he broke off to taunt.

'No, I didn't!' she denied, snapping her face taut.

'Pity, it could be much more amusing if you smiled.'

'I don't want it to be amusing! I want to get out. And stop using that ridiculously seductive accent.'

'*Is* it seductive?'

'No.'

'Pity. I was quite enjoying myself. You still wish to scream?' he asked hopefully.

'No.'

'Because I know some truly remarkable ways to stifle one.'

'I just bet you do,' she snapped crossly. Pressed up against a shelf which was digging painfully into her shoulder blades, she held her hands out in warning.

'Francine,' he murmured. It sounded as though it were a name he were savouring. Easily evading her hand that tried to knock his aside, he trailed his fingers across her cheek. 'Francine.'

'Don't keep saying that!' Jerking her head aside, she stared fixedly at a broom handle.

'But I like it.'

'Well, I don't like you saying it!'

'Named by your godmother, presumably, seeing as you are English.'

'Yes! And you can't really be arrogant enough to think that I'll melt into your arms after all the things you've said to me, accused me of, *treated* me to!'

'Only because I thought you were Cecille.'

'I don't care if you thought I was Cleopatra! You still said them!'

'So I did.'

'And aren't you forgetting Claire?' she asked desperately.

'Who?' he asked lazily.

'Stop it! Just stop it! You really expect me to forget the way you've behaved? Scowling, reproving, not to say downright insulting...'

'I never scowl.'

'One minute evil,' she continued determinedly, 'the next as nice as pie.'

'Apple?'

'What?' Thrown off balance for a minute, she almost stamped her foot. 'Any pie you like! And I won't forget it! Don't want to forget it! And at the earliest opportunity, I shall leave, return home, and forget I ever met you! So until that time—and stop smiling, damn you!— I should be enormously grateful if you would ignore me as I intend to ignore you! And furthermore,' she added

in fury, 'you can have all your presents back! Go and give
them to Claire—or Cecille!'

A sardonic smile on his mouth, a rather dangerous
glitter in his eyes, he drawled, 'Are you always this inconsistent?'

'*Me?*' she practically screeched. '*Me? I'm* not the one
who's inconsistent!'

'*Non?*'

'*Non!*'

Dodging past him, she wrenched open the door, and
fled. He fled silently behind her, tapped her on the
shoulder as she fought to open her bedroom door.

Whirling on him in fury, she ordered, 'Leave me
alone!'

He smiled, leaned against the wall beside her. 'But I
might want you to make me a tie-pin.'

'Shut up,' she gritted. 'Just shut up!' Shoving open her
door, she slammed it in his face, and heard him chuckle.

She didn't sleep. She *always* slept. And she didn't think
she had ever hated anyone more!

There were no trains, she was informed when she enquired next morning. The clerk looked desolate, but there
were no trains. Well, she could cope with Giles for the
few hours it would take to get to Weeson, which, if she
remembered rightly, was where he was leaving the train
to go skiing. She could manage a few hours, couldn't
she?

Entering the breakfast room, immediately spotting him
seated at a table alone, she jerked her head away, but not
before she'd seen his sardonic smile, the way he half rose,
bowed to her. Thankfully seeing her grey-haired companion, whose name she *still* didn't know, she joined
him, chatted inconsequentially about the ball, glossed
over her reasons for leaving so abruptly without saying

good-night; chatted brightly about the journey ahead of them, despite the intrigued twinkle in his blue eyes, and then it was time to go. Horse-drawn sleighs took them back to the station, and to their own train rescued from the avalanche. To her surprise, neither Marguerite nor her husband were with them. Not sufficiently interested to wonder why, she didn't ask.

Wandering into the lounge, she smiled at the steward, asked after Jean-Marc, and was told that after treatment at the local hospital, Giles had arranged for him to be flown home. Not wishing to discuss Giles, she asked for a coffee, then sat sipping and watching the scenery. Mostly people were quiet after their late night, or hung over, but it was a friendly quiet, satisfied.

'Heidi country,' Giles murmured softly as he slid into the seat beside her, and she stiffened, refused to look at him. 'Where her crippled friend Clara came searching for a cure for her paralysis.'

Ignoring him, but not quite able to ignore the warmth of his body pressed to hers, she stared fixedly at the scene outside.

'And there,' he continued, reaching across her to point, his arm deliberately, or accidentally, brushing her breast, 'is the Falknis peak. See the skiers?'

Yes, I can see the skiers, she wanted to snap. Not being blind, I can see them perfectly well.

'Not going to forgive me?' he asked softly. 'Not ever going to let me kiss you again? Hold you in my arms?'

Shocked, she snapped round to glare at him, then wished she hadn't. Grey eyes were much too close. His mouth was much too close, and she dragged in a sharp breath, turned quickly away. And the train, indifferent, rattled on its way. Soon, she kept telling herself desperately, in half an hour, an hour, he would be gone.

'You stayed with Mally a lot? Loved her? Looked after her?' Long fingers touched her hair, moved an errant wisp aside, and she shivered, closed her eyes, prayed for common sense.

'I was in danger of forgetting that life is for living, I think. That it's precious, that laughter is as important as diligence. I want to laugh with you, Francine.'

And if she didn't move soon, get away from him, she was in danger of forgetting how he'd treated her. In danger of succumbing to a charm that was pervasive—and erratic. 'Is that what you say to Claire?' she taunted, and was horrified to discover how husky her voice sounded. She expected him to stiffen, become angry, but he didn't.

'Claire is gone. Never to return. Claire was a mistake. Claire, and all the Claires like her, would never have bandaged a barman's hand; would never have helped an old lady up from the floor; obeyed orders when she'd just been insulted. Would not have thought to organise tea for shock. You saw me with Claire in Paris.'

'Saw you arguing.'

'Yes. She had just informed me that she would not be coming on the trip. Had no desire to act as hostess for the bourgeoisie. That she'd had a better offer.'

'Greek millionaire.'

He smiled. 'Mm.'

'But you're a millionaire.'

'Mm. But not a jealous one. Not for Claire, anyway.'

'You were supposed to plead?'

'Mm.'

'And you didn't.'

'No. I might plead with you,' he whispered softly, and she swallowed hard.

'I don't want you to plead with me.'

'I know. I saw you arrive at the Gare de L'Est. You looked sad, a little bit lost, and then you disappeared, and I wondered, briefly, who you were, where you had gone, what train journey you would be on, never for a moment thinking you would be on mine.'

'And when you did see me, here, in the lounge, you thought me an interloper.'

'No. I thought you Cecille, because I had asked the steward who you were, and he said your ticket was marked for Madame Marie-Louise Patry. And so, because of the letter, because I had misread her handwriting, I thought you Cecille.'

'Yes.'

'And last night, I was angry, because I felt something I did not want to feel—for Cecille. A Cecille who cried at the sound of a carol, who patted a horse's neck and smiled. Who thanked the carol singer for her time. A girl who wore a red dress to cheer everyone up.'

'I wore it to cheer myself up. In defiance, and because I had promised Mally that I would have a good time.'

'I know.'

'No,' she denied quietly, 'you don't know. Don't know me at all.'

'But beginning to learn. And wanting to learn more.'

'No.'

'Lake Walensee,' he explained automatically as he glanced through the window. 'Churfisten mountains.'

'What? Oh.' Giving the lake and the mountains beyond it a fleeting glance, and knowing that if she didn't leave now she'd probably end up making a fool of herself, *believing* him, she blurted quickly, 'Excuse me, I need something from my cabin.' Squeezing awkwardly past him, she almost ran along the train towards her sleeping compartment. She could lock herself in until he left. Seemed a bit excessive, but it might stop feelings she didn't want to feel. A wavering that would be foolish in the extreme.

As she reached her door, the motion of the train changed, the *sound* changed, and the overhead lights came on as they entered a tunnel. Stiffening, and knowing that she really didn't want to be shut in her cabin whilst they were in a tunnel, she waited. It could only be a few minutes, probably. A few minutes wouldn't make any difference. She didn't hear Giles walk up behind her, didn't even see his reflection in the window, and when he spoke, she jumped like a startled rabbit, turned, her eyes full of fear.

'Hey, hey, it's only me,' he soothed gently. Peering into her face, he asked kindly, 'What's wrong?'

Feeling stupid, she gave a nervous laugh. 'Nothing. I don't like tunnels, that's all.' And then the train began to slow, and she glanced worriedly at the dark window. 'Why is it slowing?'

'Because it does,' he reassured her. 'There's nothing to worry about.'

'No,' she agreed shakily, and then it stopped, and she clutched at the front of his sweater, listened, awaited disaster. There was a low rumble, then a whoosh, and she jumped, gave a little yelp, and Giles pulled her against him, fought not to laugh.

'Another train,' he soothed against her hair. 'Trains do pass from time to time.'

Embarrassed, she tried to straighten. 'Yes, well.' Realising what she was doing to his sweater, she hastily unclenched her hands, tried to smooth the rumpled wool.

'Clutching's OK,' he murmured on a thread of laughter. 'I like clutching.'

'Stop it,' she muttered.

Tilting her face up with one finger, he smiled down into her eyes. 'You flirted with everyone but me,' he reproved softly.

'I didn't want to flirt with you.'

'I know. Because it mattered.'

Eyes widening warily, she shook her head.

'Liar. You think I'm not experienced enough to know when there's a spark of interest?'

'I'm not interested in your experiences.'

'I'm interested in yours.'

With a despairing sigh, she tried to keep him at a distance. 'Don't do this to me. Please don't do this to me.'

'But I want to kiss you. Keep wanting to kiss you.'

'No,' she denied breathlessly.

'Yes.'

The train began to move again, and she swayed with the new rhythm. 'You're getting off soon.'

'Get off with me.'

'No. I have to go home.'

'Why?'

'Because...'

'Because you're afraid. There's no need to be, nothing will happen that you don't want to happen. And how will you ever get to know me if you keep running away?'

'I'm not running away.'

'Trying to.'

'I don't know how to ski,' she said stupidly, desperately.

'I'll teach you.'

'It will be boring for you.'

'No, it won't.'

'It's only because I'm different—'

'Uh-uh,' he reproved, placing one finger over her mouth. 'Don't accuse me of being a snob, of stepping off my lofty perch to mix with hoi polloi.'

'But your perch *is* lofty,' she pointed out with even more desperation.

'And lonely. I need a fellow eagle.'

'I don't know how to fly.'

'I do.' Bending his head, he captured her mouth with his. So very soft, so very gentle—so very persuasive.

The sigh was torn out of her, shuddered in her lungs, and when he broke the contact, she stared up at him. 'Why?'

'I don't know. Who ever knows what attracts one person to another? The shape of a nose, a voice, a gesture. I only know that I am attracted, and that I want to get to know you.'

'What happened to Marguerite?'

'Don't change the subject.'

'I *want* to change the subject!'

His mouth quirked attractively, and she felt despair wash over her. 'Gone off to get to the Greek millionaire before Claire can do so, I imagine.'

'But she has a husband!'

'Mm. And you wouldn't do that, would you, if you had a husband?'

'No.'

'Or go off with someone else's husband?' he asked carefully.

'No. Not knowing,' she added honestly.

'And was there a husband?'

'Yes. But I didn't know. I didn't,' she repeated earnestly. And she hadn't. He'd seemed so ordinary, nice, and she'd thought herself in love with him. Thought he'd been in love with her. And then his wife had turned up on

the doorstep, and she'd felt so unbelievably betrayed.
And ever since, had been so very wary of commitment.
'I thought he loved me, and he didn't, but I didn't know
he was married.'

He put a finger across her lips, nodded, believed. 'I'm
not a husband,' he said softly.

'Aren't you?'

'No.'

Finally looking up, she said stupidly. 'Your eyes are
smiling.'

'Are they?'

'Yes.'

'Probably because they have something to smile about.
Don't they? *Are* you attracted to me?'

'Yes,' she muttered. A man to die for.

'And you don't want to be hurt. You think I change my
women like I change my socks? I don't. Claire's little attempt at blackmail was because she *wasn't* my woman.'

'But wanted to be.'

'Mm. She was single, attractive, and because I dislike
entertaining, because I tend to be reclusive, I thought she
might like to act as hostess. Help the party go with a
swing. I'm not very good at swinging,' he added with a
quirky smile. 'But if you won't get off the train with me
in Weeson, then I will continue on with you back to
Paris. But there will be little chance of privacy, and I
think we need privacy. Anonymity. Unless you like to be
stared at like a goldfish in a bowl.'

She shook her head.

'Then let me—court you. Let me show you that I'm
not always arrogant, rude—reclusive. Separate rooms.
Even separate tables, if you like,' he smiled.

She shook her head again. 'Not separate tables. I don't
like to eat alone.'

'Then you will?' he asked persuasively.

Her face worried, no sign of hauteur or aloofness, just indecision, she sighed.

'Mally said it was to be my good fortune. I have to confess I thought she was being sarcastic at the time, but now... And she did tell you to have a good time. Made you promise, in fact. And perhaps this was why she wanted you to come. To meet me.'

Could it have been? Knowing Mally, it was entirely possible. A cautious smile peeped out, and he slid warm palms to frame her lovely face. 'Yes?'

'I don't...'

'Normally go off with strange men?' he asked with a smile.

'No. But if...' she added hastily.

'If you find you don't like me after all, then I give you my word that I will make it easy for you to leave. No scenes, no tantrums, no—arrogance. I will even fly you back to wherever you live. Or arrange to have someone else do so. No pressure, I promise. But it would be an awful shame not to ever know, wouldn't it?'

'Yes.'

He smiled. 'Then kiss me. A little bargain sealed.'

That funny little flutter inside, feeling suddenly shy, she rested her hands on his shoulders, raised herself on tiptoe, and pressed her mouth to his.

He allowed her about five seconds to taste him, experiment, and then he held her against him, not tight, not threateningly, and kissed her back. And this time, her sigh was blissful. Truly a man to die for. No, she mentally qualified, to live for. A man who made you want to live.

YULE TIDE

Catherine George

Chapter One

DARKNESS, driving rain and rush hour were bad travelling companions for a forty-mile drive on the day before Christmas Eve. Judith gritted her teeth as spray from passing lorries made the journey hideous on the bypass from Pennington. It was patently obvious now that she should have given the office party a miss and travelled yesterday. But yesterday she'd had no intention of spending Christmas with her brother and his family. The thought of Christmas in the bosom of Hugh and Margaret's family had been painful, pointing up her own unhappiness by the warmth that permeated the very timbers of Longhope Farm. Then today, at the height of the office revels, haunted by the letter she'd received that morning, Judith had suddenly felt lonely, utterly isolated from all the transient, seasonal jollity. The longing for family affection had been so strong she'd acted on impulse and made a brief telephone call, confessing a change of heart to her affectionate, practical sister-in-law.

Margaret had welcomed the idea with heartwarming enthusiasm, making it gratifyingly clear that the thought of Judith on her own at Christmas had been giving her nightmares, and worrying Hugh to death.

'I'm sorry, I never meant to do that! But are you sure an extra mouth to feed won't be a nuisance?' said Judith, feeling the cold core of loneliness thaw a little.

'At Christmas on a farm?' hooted Margaret. 'Besides, love, yours comes attached to a pair of willing hands.'

Margaret went on to warn about the weather. It had been the wettest December for years, and several areas of Gloucestershire were under water. The road was still passable, but in some places where it ran alongside the River Severn extreme care was necessary.

Judith refused to worry about it. The rain was sheeting down in the darkness, it was true, making driving conditions unpleasant, but her small car was reliable and she was a careful driver. The journey would just take a little longer than anticipated; something which became glaringly obvious when it took more than an hour just to negotiate the eight miles or so to the outskirts of Gloucester. Traffic was barely inching along by the time the last major roundabout was in sight, at which point Judith discovered why. The traffic police were out in force, rain dripping from bright waterproofs as they asked every driver's destination.

'Sorry, miss,' said the constable, when Judith told him she was taking the Chepstow road. 'Some parts of it are under water. Either turn back, or go into Gloucester and go on by train.'

Judith thanked him and without hesitation turned left towards Gloucester and the station. Now she'd made up her mind to go to Longhope for Christmas, she was determined to get there, however long it took. Half an hour later the car was safely stowed in a long-stay carpark, and a swift phone call ensured that Hugh would be waiting in Chepstow with the Land Rover when the train arrived.

The rain was still coming down in relentless torrents, deciding her against a twenty-minute wait outside on the platform. Judith went into the brightly lit buffet bar instead, checked the times of train arrivals on the monitor over the door, then waited in line for a cup of coffee and sat down on one of the banquettes with a gossipy tabloid newspaper someone had left behind.

Another check with the monitor a few minutes later told Judith her train was delayed by a further twenty minutes. She stared at the screen, resigned, then stiffened as the door beneath it swung open to admit a tall, heart-stoppingly familiar figure. She looked round wildly for a hiding place, but to her relief Nicholas Campion went straight to the bar without a glance in her direction. She got up stealthily and made for the exit, but Nick turned, coffee cup in hand, his eye caught by the scarlet of her raincoat. His eyes lit for an instant, then hardened as they fell to the hand she had ready on the handle of the door.

He pushed his way to her side swiftly, a sardonic eyebrow raised. 'Why, Judith! Long time no see. What brings you to this neck of the woods?'

She gave him a bright, social smile. 'Hello, Nick. I'm trying to get home.'

'Home?'

'Yes—to Longhope,' she returned evenly.

His eyes, striking as ever, narrowed to cold, blue-green slivers between his enviable lashes. 'I was told you weren't gracing Longhope for Christmas this year.' He gestured towards a pair of empty seats in the corner. 'Shall we sit down? If you're catching the Chepstow train—like me—it's delayed.'

The prospect of Nick as a fellow traveller came as a blow. But Judith sat down as he suggested, doing as he wanted, as she'd always done. Until she left him.

'I was driving,' she said, to break the heavy silence between them. 'The police told me the road's under water further on. I was advised to turn back or come here and get the train.'

'So was I.' He turned to look at her, his eyes as penetrating as ever under black hair streaked far more liberally with grey than at their last encounter. 'I chose the wrong day for a trip to Pennington.'

'Christmas shopping?' she said politely.

'No. I went to see you,' said Nick after a pause.

Judith's heart gave a great thump in her chest. She battled to keep her face blank, desperate to ask why. Instead she said casually, 'When was that?'

'Must have been about four-thirty or so.'

'You missed me by minutes.'

They looked at each other and then away, until at last she couldn't keep words back.

'Why did you want to see me?'

'To wish you a Merry Christmas, what else?' he said caustically.

She flushed angrily, and cast a longing glance up at the monitor. Ten long, endless minutes to go before the train arrived.

'You're thinner—and you've cut your hair,' he said morosely. 'I preferred it long.'

Which was why she'd had it cut. 'And yours is greyer,' she retorted.

'Hardly surprising,' he said bitterly, and silence fell again, enclosing them in a private bubble of tension in the crowded, noisy bar, until at last Nick said abruptly, 'How are you, Judith—really?'

She stared down at the black suede boots she'd given herself for Christmas. 'I'm fine. The firm is very busy. I've been promoted.'

'Congratulations.'

'Thanks. How about you? Still winging your way round the world all the time?'

Nick turned to look at her. 'Not much from now on. You must know Dad's retiring soon. I'm needed here.'

Judith raised a mocking eyebrow. 'Tethered to a desk at last? You do surprise me.'

'I rather surprised myself. But in the end I suppose I always knew it would come to that.'

'Pity you never mentioned the fact.'

'Is it?' he returned swiftly, his eyes holding hers.

'Is it what?'

'A pity. Would things have been different between us if I'd given up my globe-trotting sooner?'

'Probably not.' Judith turned away to look at the monitor. 'I'm going outside, the train's almost due.'

The windswept platform funnelled so much icy rain in the faces of the waiting passengers that when the two-carriage sprinter train finally drew in Judith was wet, half-frozen and knew she looked her worst. Her bright brown hair was cut in a bob which normally curved round her face, but the rain had plastered it flat to a face pinched with cold, her lipstick a thing of the past along with the rest of her make-up. She hadn't bothered with her face before bolting from her flat. If she'd known a meeting with Nick was likely she'd have taken more care—she scowled suddenly. Why on earth should she care what Nick thought of her appearance? His opinion didn't matter any more. As the train drew in she prayed there'd be no room for them to sit together in forced intimacy, and her prayer was answered. There was no room for either of them to sit, which made things worse, as they stood together in the midst of a heaving mass of bodies which made it impossible to avoid contact. Every bend in the track, every change of points had them bumping into each other until Judith was ready to scream. In the end Nick hooked an arm round her waist and held her tightly against him, ignoring the fulminating look she threw at him.

'Otherwise we'll both be black and blue,' he said into her ear, his breath warm against her skin as his lips brushed her lobe.

Judith clamped her teeth together to stop them chattering, hoping he'd think she was cold, instead of scorched by a visceral streak of response to his touch. Never again, she vowed bitterly, would she give way to impulse. Right now she could be warm and dry in her flat, watching television, eating her supper off a tray, enjoying a peaceful evening alone. But the picture conjured up was suddenly so unappealing she shook her head to rid her mind of it.

'Relax,' said Nick impatiently, misinterpreting the movement. 'We're not exactly strangers.'

Judith kept her head down to hide her traitorously expressive face. In the days and weeks and months after their parting she had missed a great many things she'd taken for granted during the brief, stormy period of their marriage. And this physical contact was by no means the least of them. Her cheeks burned as she thought of the nights she'd tossed and turned on the hard bed in the dreary little Pennington flat, longing for Nick's physical presence with a ferocity she'd had to learn to tame. And until now she'd honestly believed she'd managed it. They were both wearing trench-style raincoats, hers over a thick black sweater and black wool trousers, Nick, as far as she could tell, with a tweed jacket over a fawn rollneck sweater and heavy cords, yet the contact of their bodies was as unnerving as though they stood naked, skin to skin.

She ventured a glance at Nick's taut face, saw a pulse throbbing at the corner of his set mouth and with elation realised he was no more unmoved by the contact than she was.

Suddenly the train came to an unheralded stop somewhere in the Gloucestershire countryside.

'Something wrong?' asked Judith, above the hubbub of raised voices.

Nick merely shifted her in his hold more comfortably and shrugged. 'Presumably we'll soon know if there is.'

A voice over the train intercom silenced the crowded carriages, as the driver explained that the police had informed them the train could go no farther. They were at a disused halt a few miles from Gloucester. A bridge farther down the line had been weakened by flood water. Buses would come to the halt to relay passengers as far as possible by the section of road still unaffected by flooding, or those who wished could return to Gloucester with the train.

'After which,' said Nick, protecting Judith from a sudden surge of bodies as people scrambled to get out, 'I assume we walk—or swim.'

'But poor Hugh will be waiting at Chepstow for me. It's an unmanned station, he won't know what's going on,' said Judith anxiously, as Nick helped her off the train.

'I've got a phone in my briefcase. You can ring him while we wait for the buses.'

At one time Judith had detested the phone Nick was never without, resenting its intrusion into their lives. Now she blessed it, and dialled Longhope Farm by the torch Nick held for her to see.

Once Hugh was in rather flabbergasted possession of the facts he volunteered to come and fetch them as far as he could on the section of road still passable.

When Judith relayed the message Nick took the phone from her and spoke decisively to the man who was an old, valued friend as well as his brother-in-law. 'Don't set out until you hear from me, Hugh. God knows how long all this is going to take, or how far we'll get. Once we get to somewhere possible I'll ring you again. And don't worry about your baby sister; I'll take good care of her.'

It seemed a long, long time before buses arrived to rescue the wet, frozen refugees from the train. So long that Judith had no more qualms about sitting close to Nick. Once in the bus, installed in seats near the back, she was grateful for his warmth as he sat as close to her as possible.

'I only hope you don't get pneumonia after all this,' he said grimly.

'I'm pretty tough,' she said cheerfully. 'I rarely get ill.'

'I remember the isolated occasions when you did,' he said, in a tone which sent the blood rushing to her face.

It had been a private, standing joke between them that on the rare occasions she'd been given antibiotics the medication had actually heightened her responses to his lovemaking instead of damping it down. Nick had teased her about the aphrodisiac properties of the pills and taken full, relishing advantage of the situation every time.

'I wonder how far we'll get,' she said after a while, watching the rain sluice down the windows of the bus. 'The way this rain is coming down we'll need an ark to get home.'

'And I don't want Hugh stranded somewhere trying to get to us,' said Nick, frowning. 'A hardworking farmer doesn't need a fight through flood water for hours to round off his day.'

'No.' Judith sighed remorsefully. 'What a lot of trouble I'm causing. I should have stuck to my original plan and stayed in Pennington for Christmas.'

'Were you spending it with friends?' he asked casually.

Judith was tempted to lie and say yes. But it had never been easy to lie to Nick. 'No,' she said after a while. 'My aim was a peaceful Christmas all on my own. I went over to Longhope last week to deliver all the presents, and collect mine, along with a diatribe from Margaret and Hugh on the follies of my decision.'

He looked at her searchingly. 'Why didn't you want Christmas at Longhope, Judith?'

Because the previous year, so soon after the breakup, the merry-making at the large gathering Margaret always rounded up at the farm had been hard to bear. With her own unhappiness still so new and raw Judith had somehow managed to put on an act so skilful no one but Margaret had suspected she was anything but the life and soul of the party. But it had been an exhausting experience, and this year she just hadn't been able to face it. Then today the divorce papers had arrived, and anything seemed better than Christmas alone.

'We've been busy at the office,' she said elliptically. 'I rather fancied a quiet time. You know what the boys are like, and this year the baby's walking, heaven help us. But,' she added lightly, 'in the end I resorted to the female privilege and changed my mind. And landed myself in this situation, which serves me right.'

'Don't worry,' he said firmly. 'I'll make sure you get to Longhope safe and sound—even if we have to get Hugh out with the tractor to rescue us.'

Judith managed a laugh. 'Sounds like a good idea. By the way,' she added, 'where are you spending Christmas?'

Nick hesitated fractionally. 'Friar's Haven.'

Judith stared at him, surprised. 'But your mother and father are in the Caribbean. I—I had lunch with them last Sunday before they left.'

'No need to sound so guilty,' Nick said sardonically. 'I know you see them regularly.'

'It's no secret,' she retorted. 'Lydia always insisted our breakup had no affect on my relationship with her, or your father. For which I'm glad—I'm fond of them both. I don't go to Friar's Haven all that often, but I enjoy my visits very much when I do.'

'They enjoy seeing you, too, as my lady mother is at constant pains to inform me.' Nick gave a mirthless laugh. 'The way both of them behave you'd think it was I who walked out on you, not the other way round.'

The bus stopped to let some passengers out, providing a diversion, and they relapsed into silence which was easier to bear for Judith than a conversation which had no hope of leading to anything other than argument.

She leaned back in the seat wearily, reaction setting in after the shock of meeting Nick again. It was ten months since they'd last set eyes on each other, when he'd tracked her down to Longhope that last time, demanding to see her. The interview had been bitter, stormy, and final, and Nick had driven away from the farm at a speed which threatened damage to his Lotus on the rutted farm track leading to the road. And now here they were, thrown together again by something as prosaic as the weather.

Judith stole a look at the familiar, aquiline profile of the man beside her, then turned to gaze out into wet darkness only sporadically relieved by a streetlight or two as they passed the odd cluster of houses along the route. The bus stopped at intervals to let more passengers out, until at last they were the sole occupants left on board.

She stared out blindly, her first real meeting with Nick still as clear in her mind as the night Hugh brought him home to dinner unexpectedly, confident that Margaret, as always, would have no problem in catering for an extra guest. Hugh Long had been away at school with Nick Campion. Then Hugh had gone off to agricultural college in Cirencester, and Nick to take a degree in electronics engineering at Edinburgh University. But Nick's true *metier* lay in marketing, and he travelled far and wide to sell the various electronic products of the family company. And to Judith that first night at dinner, in the huge warm kitchen of the farm where she'd been born, Nicholas Campion had seemed like a glamorous stranger from another planet.

She'd known Nick Campion vaguely, of course, as she knew a lot of Hugh's friends. His parents lived only a few miles away in one of the loveliest houses in the area, and quite apart from George Campion's success in business, his wife was well known for her charity work. But Nick, like Hugh, was ten years Judith's senior, and socially she'd never been in his orbit until that fateful night. She was fresh from college with her degree in accountancy, had landed herself a fairly menial job with a firm of chartered accountants in Pennington, just to start with until she found something more to her taste, and felt on top of the world.

Judith had known she looked good that night. Her hair, longer then, had hung heavy and shining to her shoulders, and her yellow sweater had brought out gold glints in her hazel eyes. And the unexpected visitor had appreciated the effect, she'd known from the start. Hugh had been delighted when his old friend met with such a warm welcome, but only Margaret had been alive to the electric current that flowed across the table between the dark, charismatic Nick Campion and her glowing young sister-in-law.

At the time Nick had been based for a while at the Gloucester headquarters of the firm, and Judith, heady with the triumph of her new job, and living away from home for the first time, had been flattered when Nicholas Campion embarked on a campaign of such determination to conquer she'd never really had a chance. By the end of their third evening together Judith was fathoms deep in love. And miraculously, or so it seemed to her, Nick reciprocated her feelings in full.

At the time Nick's home was a small, eighteenth-century cottage in the oldest, most sought-after part of Pennington, the town which had become a fashionable spa more than two hundred years earlier. There was no privacy in the flat Judith shared with two other girls, and she soon took to spending more and more time with Nick at his house. From the first time he kissed her they were both shaken by their physical response to each other, but Judith refused to move in with him as he urged.

'No,' she'd said positively. 'I promised myself I'd never do that until—well, until I knew it would be for good.'

'You mean marriage?'

'Not necessarily. I think I mean commitment.' With superhuman effort she'd torn herself from his arms, to stand a little way away, trembling at the heat in his translucent eyes. 'It's too soon—too sudden.'

To her surprise Nick had acquiesced with a lack of argument which quite deflated her. From then on for a week or two he made no demands other than kisses and caresses which drove her frantic with longing. But he never suggested taking her to bed, nor did he bring up the subject of living together. If he'd been less attentive Judith would have thought he'd gone off the idea. But he sent flowers to the flat, to the envy of her roommates, bought her subtle little presents, books, a favourite record, a piece of old, fragile porcelain from one of the antique shops Pennington was famed for. He took her to the local theatre, out to dinner in expensive restaurants, even joined her for the family Sunday lunch Hugh and Margaret liked her to go back to Longhope for at regular intervals.

How clever he'd been, thought Judith sombrely as the bus made its slow progress through the dark, rain-swept countryside. Nick had given her precious little choice when he announced one night that this state of affairs couldn't go on. They were adults well past the age of consent, and either they became lovers or they called it a day. How confident he'd been of her reaction. Unable to bear the thought of life without him, she let him take her to bed there and then.

Once they were naked together in his wide bed the conflagration which consumed them both was so fierce Judith had no chance to inform Nick of something which by that stage seemed irrelevant to her. Nick, however, finding that he was the first lover she'd ever had, and too lost in the throes of his own desire to call a halt, told her in no uncertain terms afterwards that he should have been told.

'Why?' she'd asked, still trembling with reaction to her first experience of love, which, intense though it had been, had ended too quickly for her and left her on edge.

Nick had raised himself on an elbow to look down at her, his face still taut with need. 'Because, idiot child, I'd have taken the necessary precautions. Events rather overtook me at the last—like a bloody fool I forgot to ask the requisite question.'

'I can't take the pill,' she said baldly, 'if that's what you mean. Margaret thought I should when I went to college, but no matter what kind they tried on me I got migraines. Besides, my school was pretty hot on frightening lectures about the various dangers involved.' She gave him a long, glittering look. 'And I never met anyone who made it seem worth the risk. Until now.'

At which point Nick had taken her in his arms and begun to kiss her again, with a possessive intensity which led swiftly and inevitably to a conclusion which this time took Judith to such heights of pleasure she was speechless when at long last—Nick, the expert lover, very much in control second time round—it was over.

'Are you never going to say anything again?' he'd asked lazily, some time later.

Judith turned heavy, glittering eyes on him and smiled a smile as old as Eve. 'I was just thinking how amazing it is that I've never done this before. If I'd known what I was missing I'd have succumbed to sin long ago!'

Whereupon Nick's eyes had darkened and he held her in a bruising grip and made it gratifyingly clear there was to be no other man in her life from that moment on.

They were married a month later, just eight weeks from the night Hugh had brought him to Longhope for dinner. But marriage wasn't quite the happy ending Judith had envisaged. Due to an unconquerable fear of flying, and her determination to keep on with her job, she refused to travel with Nick sometimes as he asked in the beginning, which meant a lot of time spent alone, including both their wedding anniversaries. When he missed the second one by a day, he came home from a

trip to Japan to find his wife and most of her personal
possessions were missing.

'I'm leaving, Nick,' she'd written in the note he found
on the hall table. 'I refuse to be the little wife, waiting for
the lord and master to come home and spare a little time
for her. Try to understand. I badly need to be myself as
well as Mrs. Nicholas Campion. There's no other man
involved. There never has been from the moment I met
you. Nevertheless I can't go on like this. I'm sorry.'

She had left the note unsigned. It seemed inappropri-
ate to put 'love, Judith.' She wished she had now. She'd
never admitted it to a soul, but the sole purpose of her
move had been a kind of test for him, to show him she
had a say in the way their life was run. She'd been so
confident her departure would show Nick things had to
change between them to survive. But Nicholas Campion
had pride. Pride which after the first, inevitable series of
showdowns, wouldn't allow him to keep running after the
wife who'd left him. And after a while it was pride which
kept Judith from going back. He made no move to contact her after that final, furious departure from
Longhope, though Judith lived through the ensuing days
in constant hope of hearing his deep, unmistakable voice
on the phone, or seeing him appear outside the office
when she was ready to go home.

Only home was no longer the pretty, elegant little
house near the Pump Rooms, but a poky little attic the
other end of town, the only place she could afford now
her salary was all she had to live on. Hugh and Margaret
had been astonished by her behaviour, she knew, Hugh
demanding to know if Nick had ill treated her in any way,
Margaret asking at first if another woman was involved,
then later if Judith had found another man she preferred to Nick.

Since Judith couldn't imagine preferring any man in the world to Nick, despite everything, she managed to convince her brother and his wife that the fault was hers, that marriage with Nick was not what she'd expected it to be and that she needed to live a life of her own, rather than a half-life that was merely an extension of her husband's. And after Nick's third, abortive attempt to change her mind, she even moved to another flat.

'Nick's bound to ask me where you are. Do I give him your address?' Hugh had demanded, finding the entire situation hard to comprehend.

'If he wants it,' said Judith casually. 'I'm not hiding from him.'

But she might just as well have been, because Nick could have vanished from the face of the earth for all she saw of him for a while. Then one day she caught a glimpse of him in the town, coming out of the shop where he sometimes bought clothes, and on several occasions after that felt sure she saw his Lotus drive down the street where she lived. But if Nick was driving he didn't stop. Just one glimpse of him, even of the same make of car, was enough to show up the life she'd chosen for the arid desert it had become without Nick. And at last a sadder, wiser Judith became resigned to the fact that she'd lost her desperate gamble to reshape their marriage.

Much to her surprise Judith came to terms in time with her life as a single woman again, but in the limbo of a marriage that was no longer a marriage she refused all invitations from other men. Though when word was out that she was separated from Nick these came thick and fast at first. It was Nick's mother who kept her up to date with his whereabouts and the constant round of travels he embarked on after the rift. The Campions were astonished and deeply upset by it, at first convinced that their son was to blame. Even though Judith assured them he was not, that it had been her choice to leave him, Lydia Campion harboured deep suspicions that Nick had been unfaithful to his bride. Without telling her the entire story Judith finally convinced his mother that this was untrue. But no one other than Nick, Judith felt, needed to know all her reasons for walking out on what their friends and family had believed to be the perfect marriage.

Chapter Two

'THAT was a heartfelt sigh,' said Nicholas Campion, and put a hand over hers. 'Don't worry, Judith, I'll get you back to Longhope eventually.'

'Yes, of course,' she said lightly, withdrawing her hand, then regretting it as she felt him stiffen. 'At least we can both swim.'

'It won't come to that, I promise.' He sat up, peering ahead of him at the road. 'We're slowing down—I'll just have a word with the driver.' He jumped to his feet as the bus stopped and a traffic policeman climbed on board.

After some rapid consultation with both men Nick came back to Judith and took his briefcase and her overnight bag from the rack. 'End of the line, I'm afraid. From here on we're on our own.'

Judith smiled at him philosophically. 'Perhaps someone will lend us a boat,' she said, as the policeman helped her off the bus.

'Don't accept, madam, even if they do,' advised the constable in alarm. 'The Severn's a tidal river, you could get swept away as far as the Bristol Channel. It's an estuary—anything could happen.'

'It's all right, Officer,' said Nick, jumping down after tipping the bus driver. 'My wife was joking. She was born in the area.'

'That's all right then, sir.' The man smiled. 'We've been busy enough as it is, rescuing people from stranded cars, without worrying about boats. Careful as you go, sir, it'll be high tide soon.'

Nick assured him they wouldn't add to the worries of the police force, slung Judith's bag over his shoulder, and took the torch from his briefcase. She took charge of the latter, then held on to his arm as ordered as they started off on the next stage of their journey.

'Apparently,' Nick said, as they walked along a narrow middle section of road still above water, 'from a hundred yards or so further on it's under water. According to the constable it can be waded through with care, until we reach Barnford. Luckily the town rises steeply from the river, and we can get up the main street without much problem. Unfortunately, once past the church the road dives down to the river again and apparently disappears underwater for a fair stretch.'

Judith shivered at the prospect. 'We should have gone back on the train,' she said bitterly. 'Would you have pressed on like this if I hadn't been so set on it?'

'No,' he said frankly, coming to a halt as the road suddenly became a river. 'I'd have gone back to Gloucester and put up at a hotel.'

'Are you saying you've landed yourself in this ridiculous situation just because I was determined to get to Longhope tonight?' she demanded incredulously.

'Yes,' he said simply. 'I'm learning slowly, Judith. In the past I would have insisted you went back with me, overruled your refusal, ridden roughshod over any objections you had. But I've had time—far too much of it— to rethink my attitude where you're concerned, so tonight I did what you wanted.'

'Which means you're soaked through to the skin, probably hungry, and before there's any hope of food, shelter, or even Hugh riding to the rescue on his tractor, we've got to get through this lot.' She began to laugh.

'What's so funny?' he demanded, his grip tightening on her arm.

'Nothing, really,' she gasped. 'It's just that I've often pictured meeting up with you again, but my wildest dreams never came up with a scenario like this!'

He began to laugh with her, and for a moment they stood together in the pouring rain in the darkness, the sheer discomfort and unlikelihood of the situation suddenly absurd rather than potentially dangerous.

After a while Nick shone the torch at the waterlogged route stretching away in front of them, then bent his head towards hers. 'Well? Do we go on, or try and get back to some pub still on dry land and hope we can find shelter for the night?'

'And admit defeat?' she said valiantly. 'Certainly not. A pity I'm wearing my beautiful new boots; nevertheless I vote we press on.'

'Right. Whatever you say.'

Gingerly they began to wade on along the road through water that was shallow at first, but gradually grew deeper. They were able to judge the depth by the odd car which had been abandoned along the route, but after a while there was nothing but wind and rain lashing the trees along the road and the fathomless black water ahead which gave a strange feeling of disorientation, making it hard to tell where the road merged into the river. At that point Nick insisted on going first.

'Hook your hand into my belt,' he ordered, 'but try not to cannon into me if I make an emergency stop. You're a lot shorter than me, so give a tug if you feel you're getting out of your depth.'

Judith held on to the belt like grim death as they moved cautiously forward, hugging the side nearest the trees on the right. She gritted her teeth, determined to carry on as long as possible, even though by this stage it was difficult to know whether she was out of her depth or not. Her feet and legs had lost all feeling shortly after the icy water crept higher than her knee-length boots. She comforted herself that this stretch of road was short, and by the faint orange glow from streetlights in the distance it wasn't far to Barnford, where the road would take them up a steep hill through the town.

After agonisingly slow progress for what seemed like hours she felt the water rise to thigh level and gasped, filled with a sudden vision of high tide and the river sweeping in to engulf them. Nick stopped dead.

'Are you all right?' he demanded roughly.

'Fine!' she assured him through chattering teeth. 'Well, not fine, exactly—sort of as well as can be expected.'

'We've reached the point of no return,' he said, breathing heavily, 'but if you can manage to wade through the next few yards the road will start to rise.'

'Three cheers.' She gave a hoarse little chuckle. 'Lead on, MacDuff.'

His answering laugh was carried off on the wind, as slowly, painfully, wondering if she'd drown or die of exposure first before they reached high ground, Judith struggled manfully through the water until to her horror it reached her hips. Then Nick stopped again.

'Can you hang on there for a minute or two, Judith?'

'Why?' she demanded, panicking.

'I'm going to press on and deposit this bag of yours somewhere, then come back for you.'

'Don't leave me! Let the bag go, for heaven's sake,' she gasped, suddenly at the end of her tether.

Nick shone the torch in her face, and without a word abandoned the bag to the flood water. Then he handed her the torch and lifted her in his arms. 'You light the way, I'll do the rest.'

'But, Nick—' she protested involuntarily.

'This time I *am* riding roughshod over you,' he said, panting, 'now just shut up and let me bloody well get on with it.'

After a gruelling few minutes, during which Judith was sure at times that Nick was in danger of dropping her, he deposited her on the pavement which shone above the water under the first streetlight of Barnford. There was a wooden railing lining a sodden grassy bank before the first buildings came into view, and for a moment or two they leaned against it, exhausted. Judith shivered uncontrollably, her teeth chattering like castanets, while Nick breathed in heavy, laboured gasps as he took a minute or two to recover. Then he caught Judith by the arm and hauled her along the pavement and up the hill through the rain-swept, deserted town, past shops with a Dickensian aura about their bow-fronted, tinsel-decked windows.

'It's so quiet,' gasped Judith, wondering if she'd ever feel warm again, even if she survived the pneumonia she was now convinced would overtake them both.

'No traffic,' Nick panted. 'The town's cut off from the main road.'

Suddenly a large figure emerged from a shop doorway and confronted them both. 'Good evening.'

The bobby in his archaic helmet was like a vision from heaven. 'Good evening, Constable,' said Nick, breathing heavily. 'We've just waded through the flood waters back there.'

The constable expressed his concern in no uncertain terms as a streetlight illuminated Judith's white, exhausted face and soaked condition. 'Where are you trying to get to, sir?'

'The lady wants to get to Little Mynd, to Longhope Farm.'

'Not much hope of that, madam. It's not flooded in that particular area, but several parts of the road are under water before you get anywhere near it.'

'We need to ring my brother,' broke in Judith urgently, then realised that the briefcase was as sodden as the rest of her. 'But I think I've drowned your phone, Nick,' she added unsteadily.

'If you'll just come along to the police station up the hill, sir, madam, you can make a phone call from there, and I could find out if the Bull could put you up. They don't take visitors as a rule—'

'Thank you, Constable, that won't be necessary,' said Nick, as he almost dragged Judith up the hill, and her heart sank. At the thought of wading their way along twelve miles or so of waterlogged road she wanted to lie down and die. 'Is there a taxi available?' he went on, to her astonishment.

'There is, of course, sir,' said the policeman blankly, 'but not much point asking Ernie Miller to send one of his cabs out tonight with the flood water up so high. In the morning, when the tide's turned, he might be able to get a car through, but I wouldn't count on it.'

'I meant a trip past the church and over the Ridgeway to Upper Highfield.' Nick smiled at the constable as they reached the police station. 'The road's steep and probably hellish muddy after this lot, but there's certainly no danger of flooding. My parents live up there.'

The constable nodded vigorously, patently pleased that he could do something to help. 'That's different, sir.'

Judith was made much of in the small police station, given steaming hot tea and a dry towel for her hair, and exclaimed over for her pluck in braving the flood. She felt guilty, and totally undeserving, deeply conscious that it was her own pigheadedness in wanting to get to Longhope that had landed them in the mess in the first place. It had never occurred to her that Nick had come along purely for the ride, to make sure she arrived in one piece. Which she had. Not to Longhope, it was true, and in a sorry, sodden state, but definitely in one piece due to Nick's considerable exertions. She waited apathetically, wondered if she'd ever feel warm again as Nick made a brief phone call to Hugh, promising to ring again once they arrived at Friar's Haven. And then the taxi arrived, and there was a flurry of good nights and compliments of the season, and she was wrapped in a rug in the back of a mercifully warm car and they were on their way past the church and up the winding road which led to the house where Nick had been born.

As the taxi drove away Nick unlocked the door, turned on lights and ushered Judith into Friar's Haven. The low-ceilinged hall was square and welcoming, with oils of country scenes on the panelled walls, and in the angle of the staircase a tall Christmas tree, with lights which winked among the brilliant baubles on its branches as Nick flicked a switch. But to Judith the most important feature of all was the wonderful, life-giving warmth.

'A case of Hobson's choice for accommodation,' said Nick expressionlessly. 'Under the circumstances this was the only place possible. Just for the night, of course.'

Judith knew she was in no position to mind. She nodded briefly, standing where she was just within the doorway. 'I didn't think of Friar's Haven. I never knew there was another way up here, I've only come the direct way from Gloucester.'

'Don't just stand there making polite conversation,' he said impatiently, 'go up to my mother's bathroom and run the water as hot as you can bear it. Borrow whatever you want from her wardrobe.'

'Thank you,' she said politely. 'Perhaps you could take my raincoat and boots and put them in the kitchen, or somewhere, to drip.'

Nick nodded brusquely as he stripped off his trench coat. 'Right. Get them off, then.'

'I'm afraid,' said Judith, in a faint, detached voice, 'that I don't seem quite able to. . .'

He gave her a swift, narrowed look, then sprang across the beautiful, faded Persian carpet and steadied her as she began to sway. 'Don't pass out on me,' he rapped at her.

Judith clenched her teeth, swallowing hard, and with superhuman effort managed to pull herself together. 'Sorry,' she gasped. 'Must be the warmth—after the cold. I feel a bit sick.'

'You'll feel better once you've got these wet things off,' said Nick, wrenching buttons from their moorings as he stripped off her raincoat. He thrust her down on a carved bench against one wall. 'Sit down. I'll pull your boots off.'

This was easier said than done and took more effort than either of them found easy by this time. Nick, Judith noted numbly, looked white and exhausted after their ordeal. And if Nick, who took pride in keeping fit, looked so ghastly, *she* probably looked like the ghost of Christmas past. Judith was not given much to exercise, apart from a short walk to and from the office, and in summer the odd game of tennis. From now on, she vowed silently, panting as she struggled to help Nick remove the second stubborn, knee-length boot, she would do aerobics, run miles every day and watch less television. Next time she coped with a flood she'd make sure she was fighting fit for it.

'Done,' panted Nick, and hauled her to her feet. Unfortunately he let her go quickly, and Judith collapsed in a clumsy little heap on the floor.

'Sorry,' she muttered, embarrassed, as he pulled her to her feet again. 'Feet and legs a bit numb.'

'Hardly surprising!' Nick eyed her sodden, high-heeled boots disparagingly. 'Your taste in shoes still as frivolous as ever, I see.' He held her steady by the elbows then shrugged impatiently. 'I'll give you a lift upstairs, but after our recent exertions I'm afraid it won't be very elegant.' And without warning he heaved her over his shoulder like a sack of potatoes and started up the stairs with her, panting as though she weighed a ton.

He marched along the hall and into his parents' bedroom, turning on lights as he went. By the time he deposited his burden on a stool in the adjoining bathroom he was breathing like a marathon runner, and Judith sported two hectic spots of colour in the face which had been hanging over Nick's shoulder.

Without a word Nick turned on the hot tap, then stood, eyeing her. 'Can you manage?'

'Yes!' she said hastily. 'I'll be fine. See to yourself, please. You're just as wet as me.'

'Right!' He hesitated for a moment, then strode from the room, shutting the door behind him rather loudly.

Lydia Campion liked her creature comforts. Choosing from several flagons of bath oil on a shelf above the bath, Judith emptied something smelling of spring flowers into the hot water, then not without some difficulty managed to strip off her sodden clothes. She climbed gingerly into the gleaming white tub and sent up a prayer of thanksgiving for having reached safety. Her brain must have been as waterlogged as the road, she thought morosely, as she let herself down into the water, because it had never once occurred to her, during the difficult progress through the flood, that Friar's Haven was the obvious place to make for if they couldn't get to Longhope. For a while she endured minor agony as the blood began to flow in her arms and legs again, but once the painful, tingling period was over she felt her entire body relax as the heavenly warmth permeated through it. She lay back in mindless bliss, refusing to think of what was next on the agenda, once she was forced to get out of the water and face Nick again. It was too complex a problem for the moment. Her brain just couldn't cope with it. Besides, she thought, yawning, it wasn't such an insurmountable problem. In the morning she would probably, some way or other, be able to go on to Longhope.

It was the last conscious thought Judith had for some time until violent banging on the door woke her from a doze.

'Are you all right?' yelled Nick. 'I didn't go through all that out there to have you drown in the bath, Judith!'

'I'm fine,' she said, spluttering as water lapped at her mouth. 'I'll just wash my hair, then I'll be out.'

A few minutes later, wrapped in Lydia Campion's white towelling robe, wet hair brushed back under a swathing towel, Judith emerged into the bedroom to raid her mother-in-law's belongings. She stopped short as she found Nick standing there waiting for her, dressed in a heavy sweater and comfortable old cords, his arms folded and his long legs apart in a stance she remembered only too well.

'*Are* you all right?' he demanded.

'Yes,' she said breathlessly, suddenly so illogically shy her face flamed under the swathing white towel. 'I—I was just coming to find something to wear.'

'I was worried,' he said in a constricted voice. 'You looked like a ghost downstairs.'

'I felt like one.' She gave him a bright, social smile, conscious that the camaraderie between them was missing now they'd won through to safety.

'I'll get us something to eat,' said Nick gruffly, and turned towards the door.

'Nick,' said Judith quickly. 'Wait! I haven't thanked you for rescuing me. The water was so deep in one place I panicked.'

He turned, a quickly veiled gleam in his eyes. 'I know. I still tune in to your vibrations—some of them, anyway. I suppose you'd have drowned rather than admit you couldn't go any further.'

'Of course not! Besides, I *can* swim, remember.'

'I do remember. But you were cold and exhausted. I don't think you'd have found it easy.'

'I know I wouldn't—which is why I'm saying thank you.' She moved towards him and touched his arm, her smile warmer. 'I bet Sir Walter Raleigh wasn't so hard to thank when he threw his cloak down for Queen Elizabeth.'

Nick stood very still, then moved abruptly, shaking off her arm, and dismayed, Judith dodged back, the towel sliding off her hair with the movement. They snatched at it simultaneously, bumping into each other awkwardly in the process, and Nick smothered a curse and jerked her into his arms, kissing her with the explosive hunger her body remembered and responded to before she could control it. She gasped, her mouth opening under his, but when his tongue came seeking in instant, hot demand, Judith came to her senses with a jolt and pulled free, her entire body consumed with heat.

'I suppose you expect an apology,' said Nick through clenched teeth, but she shook her head.

'No. It was—I know you didn't—I mean, we've been through a lot tonight—'

'Which was no excuse. I apologise,' he said, with sudden, chilling formality. 'When you come downstairs I'll have something ready to eat.'

Judith raised her head and looked him straight in the eye. 'How kind,' she said distantly. 'I admit I'm hungry. I haven't eaten since breakfast.'

'Since when did you start eating breakfast?' he said sardonically.

'Since I left you,' she said brutally. 'A lot of things changed in my life at that point.'

'One thing hasn't changed.' He walked to the door, arrogance in every line of him. He turned and gave her a smile which curled her bare toes into the pile of his mother's bedroom carpet. 'Your response to me is the same as ever.'

'Only the same?' countered Judith sweetly. 'I hoped it might have been better. I feel I've honed my skills in that direction somewhat since we last met, Nicholas. Once it was known we were no longer together, offers of consolation came in thick and fast.'

If she'd hoped for reaction, she was disappointed. Nicholas Campion, as she should have remembered, was adept at hiding his feelings.

'Hardly surprising,' he said without expression. 'Don't be long. I'm heating some soup.'

Judith watched him leave, cursing herself for giving in to childish retaliation. It was true that she'd had offers enough, but she'd lied about accepting them. Yet Nick hadn't taken the news with quite the imperturbability he'd pretended. He'd utterly failed to control the familiar, tell-tale throb at the corner of his mouth, giving the lie to his indifference.

Chapter Three

FOR a century before George Campion bought Friar's Haven for his bride it had been a monastic retreat. These days its atmosphere was definitely secular, yet a certain sense of peace still lingered. Added to Lydia Campion's skill for homemaking the house exuded a welcome over and above the physical warmth which George Campion grumbled at good-naturedly, due to the size of the heating bills.

In the kitchen, which was very much of the present day, with a plethora of gadgets to indulge Lydia's love of cooking, the peace was less in evidence by the time Judith finally arrived there to join Nick. She hesitated in the doorway, conscious of looking odd in her borrowed plumes. Lydia was both taller and more angular than her son's wife, and Judith had been hard put to find something suitable to wear. In the end she'd resorted to a heavy red sweater from her father-in-law's shelves to wear with a narrow black jersey skirt of Lydia's, which though it reached to Judith's ankles, had enough give in the knitted material to make it comfortable. There had been several pairs of Lydia's favourite sheer dark tights available, though the only possible footgear had been a pair of backless black velvet mules trimmed with ostrich feathers.

'Sorry to be so long,' she said awkwardly, as Nick glanced up from the pan of soup he was stirring.

He looked her up and down, his lips twitching as his eyes lingered on her feet. 'Dad must have bought my mother those.'

Judith smiled a little. 'Can I do anything to help?'

'You could make coffee. Mother's the only one privy to the mysteries of the coffee maker.'

'We could always have instant,' she suggested, examining the appliance warily.

'My taste in coffee is just the same as it always was,' he said shortly, pouring soup into two bowls. 'I like the real thing—or nothing.'

Their eyes met, and Judith returned to the coffee machine hurriedly. 'Surely an engineer can operate one of these?'

'This one just doesn't feel equal to the task after the adventures of the evening.' He strolled to the table with the bowls of soup, and set them down on the scrubbed wooden table alongside a platter of thickly sliced bread. A dish of butter and a plate with two kinds of cheese completed the array, and Judith abandoned the coffee maker, suddenly too hungry to bother with its complexities.

'I'll make tea afterwards instead,' she said decisively, and sat down in the chair Nick pulled out for her. 'Mm, smells good. What is it?'

'A couple of cans of thick vegetable soup with some of that Stilton crumbled into it.' He sat down opposite and looked at her levelly. 'You were very fond of Stilton—once.'

'I still am.' Judith helped herself to bread and began on the soup with appreciation.

There was silence in the room as they emptied the bowls at speed. Nick got up at once to refill them. 'You look a lot better already,' he remarked as he sat down again.

'Amazing what a spot of food can do,' she agreed. 'The first today for me, as a matter of fact.'

'You said you ate breakfast these days,' he reminded her swiftly.

'I lied.' She shrugged. 'I'm afraid coffee, tea and a mouthful of cheap champagne is all I've had today up to now.'

'No wonder you almost passed out in the hall!' His eyes narrowed. 'Why champagne?'

'There was a party at the office.' Judith laid down her spoon and looked up. 'It had only just got underway when I found I just couldn't stand all the jollity and seasonal cheer and decided to make a dash for it back to Longhope. So I rang Margaret, whose response was far warmer than I deserve, then set off in the pouring rain at rush hour. The rest you know.'

'But didn't you hear traffic reports on the car radio while you were driving?' he asked, frowning.

'No. My car radio died recently. I'm hanging on for the sales after Christmas to buy a new one.'

'If you're short of cash why the hell won't you use some of the money I pay into your account every month?' he demanded, scowling.

Judith opened her mouth to snap back, then thought better of it. 'I am not short of money. But it seems silly to pay full price for a radio when a short wait can get me a bargain in the sales. And you know perfectly well why I won't touch your money,' she added with sudden heat.

'Just so you can show me how well you manage on your own, and how little you need me—or my money?' His eyes glittered coldly as they stared into hers, but Judith held his gaze without flinching.

'It would be singularly pointless to rattle on about being my own woman and needing a life and an entity of my own, Nicholas Campion, and then take money from the very man I'm trying to prove it all to.' She looked away, and very deliberately helped herself to some Stilton.

Nick stared at her in silence, then followed suit. 'It's not a very substantial meal to offer someone who hasn't eaten all day.'

'It's fine. Or are you still hungry?' she asked. 'I could make an omelette or something, if Lydia's left some eggs.'

'Of course she has. As you know, I've rented out our—the house in Bath Crescent. The tenants aren't moving out until next month, which made my plans uncertain for Christmas,' he said expressionlessly. 'I convinced my mother this needn't affect her holiday, but couldn't prevent her from leaving eggs, and everything else she could think of, as well as filling the freezer before they left for the Caribbean. Which explains the fresh bread. With the wonders of technology at my disposal it was easy to defrost a loaf in the microwave.'

'You weren't so domesticated at one time,' observed Judith, taking another slice of bread. In the past the merest hint of an argument would have killed her appetite, but these days, she found to her satisfaction, she was made of sterner stuff.

'I never claimed expertise in the kitchen,' he agreed smoothly, then smiled into her eyes. 'But I made up for it in the bedroom.'

'There's more to life than bed,' she returned, unmoved, and got up to fill the kettle. While it boiled she searched in the cupboards and found a carton of dried milk.

Nick got up to take the tea tray from her. 'Do you want to drink this here, or would you like to go into Mother's little sanctum?'

'Let's stay here—easier for washing up.' Judith felt she could cope with the situation better in the kitchen than in the intimacy of Lydia's small, cosy morning room. 'Jon isn't coming home this Christmas, I gather.'

Jonathan Campion was ten years younger than Nick, a smaller, irreverent version of his brother, but no less clever, and currently at Harvard Business School with a view to joining the family company when he qualified.

'Jon's staying in the States with the girlfriend, otherwise Mother and Dad might not have gone to the Caribbean. I,' he added drily, 'assured them I could look after myself for Christmas.'

'What did you do last year?' asked Judith, then wished she hadn't at the derisive look it won her from Nick.

'Is this the first time you've wondered that? Surely my parents filled you in on the trip I took to Australia, from whence I made bloody sure I wasn't able to get back for the season of good will. I wasn't feeling much good will at the time. To you, or anyone else.'

Judith drank her tea in silence, while Nick got up and fetched an unopened bottle of single malt from the kitchen counter.

'This was pressed on me at *our* office party today,' he said sardonically. 'I felt obliged to show my nose for a minute, because Dad and Jon were missing. Since one can't drink and drive these days no one thought it odd when I bowed out with the excuse of having to get back. Nor was anyone tactless enough to ask where—or who— I was getting back to. Would you care for some?'

Judith disliked whisky, but in the circumstances a stimulant of some kind seemed like a good idea for once.

'Yes, please,' she said, surprising him. 'I'll have a spot in my tea.'

'In your *tea?* You expect me to pour venerable nectar like this into hot tea?'

'Why not?'

Nick grinned suddenly, looking more like the man she'd fallen in love with. 'Why not, indeed! Say when.'

The relaxing effect of the spirit on both of them was instantaneous. Alcohol had never been one of Nick's weaknesses, Judith acknowledged as she sipped her unaccustomed drink, and certainly not one of hers. Nick had been her weakness, so much so that she'd never needed any others. And since her flight to independence the only weakness which superseded it was an occasional indulgence in chocolate. Heavens, she thought, suppressing a giggle. How dull. Not for her the balm of sexual flings with new partners. She looked at Nick with sudden curiosity, the relaxing properties of the whisky already taking effect.

'Have you had lots of other women since we split up?'

'No,' he snapped with sudden malevolence, 'I bloody well haven't. And we didn't split up, Judith. You walked out on me. It's not the same thing.'

'No,' she acknowledged, warmth beginning to rise in her pale face. 'I wouldn't blame you if you had, you know.'

'Very magnanimous,' he said scathingly. 'Now tell me about all these men you've been practising your sexual skills on.'

'I lied about that, too,' she said, unrepentant. 'You made me angry.'

'A habit of mine,' he agreed, his eyes narrowing sharply. 'Are you saying there's been no one at all?'

'Are you?'

Their eyes met and held.

'I tried,' said Nick with bitter honesty. 'If it's the truth you want, you might as well know I tried bloody hard.'

'To do what?'

'Make love to someone else—to forget you. Forget how good we were together. Forget how much I wanted you back.' He shrugged, his jaw clenched. 'Unfortunately—don't laugh—it didn't work. My libido gave up on me. On my travels I wined and dined several women at first, but after a while packed it in—even began to worry there was something seriously wrong with me. Which, of course, there was. I'd lost you, and found I couldn't raise even a flicker of desire in any other woman.' He gave a mirthless bark of laughter. 'Quite a joke!'

'I don't think it's funny,' said Judith softly, wondering if the whisky was making her feel so warm inside.

'How about you?' Nick gave her a look like an X-ray. 'Was it the same for you?'

'Not quite,' she said, trying to be accurate, and poured herself another cup of tea. Without asking, Nick leaned over and added a small quantity of Scotch. 'Are you trying to make me drunk?' she inquired.

'No. After our perils, Judith, we deserve a little medicine. Besides, two teaspoons of Scotch in a pint or so of tea won't do you much harm.'

She smiled, watching as he poured himself a shot of whisky even more sparing than the first. 'I told you I got lots of invitations from men at the office once it was known I was—well, separated from you. But I didn't accept any, for the simple reason that every man jack of them was a bit obvious about filling the vacant place in my bed.'

'And you didn't want that?' he asked, looking visibly more relaxed.

Judith downed half the aromatic contents of her teacup, frowning. 'No. Since you've been honest, I might as well admit I did miss that part of our marriage, though no more than any other part of it. I suppose what I'm saying is that I missed *you,* Nick. More than I would have believed possible after resenting the way you laid down the law so much.'

'I suppose,' he said with care, 'it never occurred to you to let me *know* you missed me?'

She shook her head. 'No way. After that final time, when you drove away from the farm in such a rage, I thought you didn't want me any more.'

'How the hell did you get promotion?' he demanded bitingly. 'Do they realise at these chartered accountants of yours what an idiot you are?'

'I am not an idiot! If you did want me back why didn't you get in touch and tell me?'

'Judith, *you* were the one who left! Sheer male pride made it imperative that you were the one who suggested coming back, dammit.' Nick swallowed the remains of his drink and glared at her. 'You seem to have forgotten that I made three attempts to persuade you—'

'*Persuade!*' she cut in, her eyes flashing with tigress glints. 'All you wanted was for me to throw in the job and settle down to being wifey to you, with no life of my own.' Her jaw set. 'Which, unless you've forgotten, I would have done. On my own terms. But you weren't having any.'

'Was it so strange to want you to myself a bit longer? You were too young to start a family,' he said flatly.

The fire died in her eyes. 'Only in your opinion.' Judith

leaned back in her chair, eyeing him levelly. 'Even now I don't understand why, Nick. We had enough money. And I was willing to give up my job on those terms.'

'Otherwise no deal. Just to be married to me wasn't enough,' he said bitterly.

'Not when you were away for weeks at a time, it wasn't. What was I supposed to do with myself while you were junketing about all over the globe?' Judith glared at him. 'If I'd had a child to look after at least I'd have had some company!'

'My mother always managed to fill her time under the same circumstances!'

'I am me, not Lydia!' Judith breathed in deeply. 'I don't know why we're going over all this again. But I've had a lot of time to think in the time we've been apart. You were less than honest with me, before we got married. And I was so much in love with you I never even thought to bring the subject of children up. I thought a child would be the natural outcome of the way we felt for each other.'

'Was I so unreasonable in asking for a period on our own together first?' he countered swiftly.

'You didn't *ask*,' she said bitterly. 'You laid down the law. I was to give up my job and concentrate on being Mrs. Nicholas Campion, and postpone a family until some nebulous distant time in the future. You were like something out of a Victorian melodrama, Nick. Without your co-operation I couldn't do much about the family bit, but when I insisted on keeping my job our brief periods together developed into serialised arguments between your business trips. Eventually I just couldn't bear it any longer. So after a second wedding anniversary on my own I took the coward's way out and left before you got back from wherever you were at the time.'

'I suppose you expected me to make a U-turn, dash after you, say come back, all is forgiven, we'll do things your way,' he said cuttingly.

Judith nodded wryly. 'Of course! That's exactly what I expected. Pathetic, really. It just shows how much I needed to grow up, doesn't it?'

Nick stared at her in silence for a long time. 'I did dash after you,' he reminded her at last. 'On three separate occasions. Twice to that bleak little attic you found for yourself, and the last time to Longhope, where I was sure Hugh would back me up, join me in trying to make you see—'

'Sense?' she cut in caustically. 'Sense being a euphemism for what *you* wanted, of course.'

'Anyway, Hugh was no help,' said Nick, avoiding a direct reply. 'When it came to the push he was your big brother, not my old friend. While I got the distinct impression Margaret would have been ready with a pitchfork if I'd tried to enlist *her* support.'

'I am singularly fortunate in my family,' said Judith drily. 'They didn't approve of my leaving you, but both of them considered I had a right to run my life as I wanted. Which didn't stop them worrying over the mess they thought I was making of it.'

Nick looked at her for a moment, then smiled crookedly. 'I suppose you know I ring Hugh regularly?'

She stared at him incredulously. 'I certainly do not—first time I've heard of it. What do you talk about?'

'You. Between Hugh and Margaret and my parents I've monitored your progress fairly closely since the separation,' he admitted, looking wary.

Storm signals flashed in the eyes fixed on his. 'You mean you were spying on me?'

'Certainly not. Merely taking an interest in the welfare of my wife.'

'I may not be your wife much longer,' she retorted, then could have bitten her tongue out at the look on his face.

'And just what,' he said menacingly, 'do you mean by that?'

Judith's chin lifted. 'I contacted a solicitor recently about a divorce. I got a letter from him this morning, with—with some information.'

'Information,' he repeated expressionlessly, his eyes staring into hers.

She looked away, shrugging, fighting to keep her voice steady. 'We're separated, anyway. I just thought I'd do a bit of research on what happens next.'

'I see,' said Nick, in the same chilling tone. 'On what grounds were you planning to get rid of me?'

Her eyes flew back to his. 'I hadn't got that far—'

'In which case,' he cut in, 'perhaps I could remind you that you did the deserting, and I did my best to persuade you to come back.' He jumped to his feet suddenly, towering over her. 'Who is he, Judith?'

She stared up at him blankly. 'The solicitor?'

'*No*—your lover. The reason you want a divorce!'

'There isn't anyone!' she said hotly.

'And you expect me to believe that?'

'Since it's the truth, yes,' she said angrily. 'Is it so hard to believe I might just not want to be married to you any more, Nicholas Campion?'

The anger drained from his face, leaving it haggard. 'It shouldn't be. You've demonstrated the fact very clearly this past year.'

They stared at each other wordlessly, the silence stretching until Judith was ready to scream.

'In the circumstances,' she said at last, 'let's hope I can get to Longhope tomorrow.'

Nick's eyes darkened alarmingly. 'Don't worry,' he said through his teeth, 'I'll get you there if it kills me.'

Judith gulped down the last of her tea, hoping he was right. Much more of this particular form of tension they generated between them and her nerves would be in tatters. Tomorrow, Nick's help or not, she'd get herself to Longhope if she had to swim there.

Chapter Four

THE tension mounted as Nick, never famous for his domestic talents, astonished Judith by insisting on helping her leave the kitchen immaculate. They worked together in a silence full of things left unsaid, until Judith was ready to scream and the kitchen was tidy enough to please even Lydia Campion, who would have been far less pleased by her son's icy courtesy as he asked Judith if she needed anything for the night.

'I should have tried to hang onto your bag,' he said brusquely, 'but my efficient mother probably keeps spare toothbrushes in her bathroom somewhere. Help yourself to anything else you need.'

'Nothing would have been dry even if you had kept the bag,' Judith pointed out coldly. 'Don't worry, I'll be fine.'

'Ah, yes, I forgot. You're used to fending for yourself these days!'

Judith paused on her way out of the kitchen. 'Tonight, Nick, I couldn't have managed without you,' she said, looking at him squarely. 'Perhaps I haven't made it clear how grateful I am for your help.'

Nick stared at her stonily for a moment. 'Don't mention it. I'd have done the same for anyone.'

The words cut Judith like a knife, but she hid the hurt deep as they mounted the stairs together, just as they'd done so often in the past. But in happier times they'd shared the large guest-room at the back of the house, and clung together in one of the single beds rather than spend the night separate from each other.

'I'm in my old room—if you need anything,' he added, so gruffly Judith knew he'd been thinking along the same lines as herself, a common enough occurrence in the past. Neither had ever had the least trouble in knowing what the other was thinking about. Agreement had been their problem, not lack of intuition.

At the head of the stairs Nick paused. 'At least you should have no problem in sleeping tonight, Judith. You must be exhausted after our action-packed efforts to get here.'

'I'm sure I'll sleep like a log,' she said mendaciously, sure of no such thing. She gave him a rather unsteady smile and Nick made a sudden, involuntary move towards her, then stopped dead as he saw her stiffen. For a moment the atmosphere crackled with such electricity Judith could hardly breathe, then he shrugged and stepped back.

'Good night, Judith.'

'Good night,' she said pleasantly, forcing herself to walk rather than run like the wind to the Campions' bedroom. She closed the door gently then sagged against it like a rag doll. Stop being so wet, she told herself crossly, and pushed herself away from the door, letting out a half-hysterical giggle. Wet! After struggling through a flood, from now on the only time she intended to get wet was in a bath full of steaming, scented water.

She found new toothbrushes in the bathroom cabinet, as predicted, and made use of one of Lydia's impressive array of night creams on her face, then went to look for something to wear to bed. Her tall, thin mother-in-law's taste in nightgowns proved remarkably frivolous, and on someone prone to curves rather than angles, positively indecent. Judith folded them back hastily in their drawer and made do with a rose satin slip cut like a camisole. Normally she wore outsize T-shirts to bed, or nothing at all. But tonight was no night for sleeping naked—only because she was cold, she told herself firmly.

The king-sized bed was comfortable, but Judith lay tense and sleepless long after the lights were out, her mind full of Nicholas Campion. What a stupid fool she'd been to mention the word divorce. The query about it had been made on impulse, and the answer to it had only con- firmed that divorce was the last thing she wanted, how- ever much she'd tried to convince herself she'd be better off without Nick. One look at him tonight had made that painfully clear. Judith sighed miserably and flung her- self over in the great bed, wondering if Nick were asleep. Why? she asked herself satirically. Fancy going along and asking if he'd like a chat? She sat up abruptly, abandon- ing any pretence of trying to sleep, and turned on the bedside light. Both bedside tables held a pile of books. From Lydia's selection Judith chose a novel set in medi- eval Flanders and settled down to read, then looked up after a page or two, her heart thumping as she heard a knock on the door.

'Come in,' she said, in a voice she hardly recognised as her own, and Nick opened the door and stood in the opening.

'Are you all right? I went to the bathroom and saw the light under your door. I thought you might be ill.'

Nick wore an old foulard dressing gown, and Judith, remembering the garment with a pang, smiled uncer- tainly, resisting the urge to pull the covers up to her chin. 'I couldn't sleep. Odd, really. I was so tired until I got into bed. Now I'm horribly wide awake. Must have been the cheese.'

'Shall I make you a hot drink?'

She smiled a little. The Nick of old hadn't been given to making hot drinks at night. He'd brought her champagne, at times. But never hot milk. 'No, thanks. I thought I'd read one of Lydia's books. Sorry I disturbed you.'

'Under the circumstances did you really believe I'd gone to sleep?' he asked, with sudden violence.

Judith's breath caught. 'I thought you might have been tired. It was a very exhausting evening.'

'In more ways than one.'

Blue eyes glittered into widened hazel ones across the room, then Nick's mouth twisted.

'Perhaps if we talked a while we might sleep.'

'It's possible,' she agreed, dry-mouthed.

'Unfortunately,' he said softly, in a tone which sent shivers down her spine, 'I don't want to talk. I want to kiss you, hold you in my arms and make love to you until you plead with me the way you used to.'

Judith stared at him woodenly, hoping he couldn't hear the thudding of her heart under the borrowed rose silk. 'Sorry. I've kicked the pleading habit.'

'Perhaps it's time *I* acquired it.' He hadn't moved. He stood there, tall and haggard and everything in life Judith wanted, but something told her this was one of the most significant moments of her life, to guard against welcoming Nick back to her bed with open arms. In the past she'd been helpless with her response. Making love together had been the cure for everything. But no longer. Any victory Nick had in mind he'd have to fight for.

'I wouldn't,' she advised into the silence which stretched between them. 'If pleas are necessary there's no point in making them. I learned that the hard way.'

Nick's jaw tightened. 'You've changed.'

'I should hope so. I'm older—and hopefully a bit wiser.'

'Are you telling me you don't want me to make love to you?'

'Not exactly,' she admitted, scrupulously truthful.

Triumph blazed on Nick's face as he crossed the room in a couple of strides. He pulled her up into his arms and held her close, his eyes so close she could see the little flecks of jade in the blue irises. 'Darling, darling, can't you see this is a miracle? The flood brought us together, and I want you, Judith.'

'Why?' she asked, her eyes unwavering on his.

'Because we're meant for each other, and you know it!' He bent his head and kissed her in the confident, conquering way she knew so well, and she lay lax in his arms and let him.

After a while he raised his head, a dangerous light in his eyes. 'No response?'

'It's been a long time, Nick,' she said quietly. 'You took me by surprise earlier. I've had time to think more clearly since. Did you really imagine a kiss or two would make me fall to pieces?'

He thrust her back against the pillow and leapt to his feet, staring down at her. 'I won't shock you with the extent of my imaginings. Nevertheless, until I saw your light I was determined to leave you in peace. But hell, Judith, doesn't it mean anything to you that you're the only woman in the world who can do this to me? None of this works with anyone else. Only with you,' he said roughly. 'For God's sake stop all this nonsense about divorce, Judith!'

'A good thing you never fancied a career in diplomacy!' She looked at him levelly. 'The leopard's still wearing the old, familiar spots, I see. All that talk about rethinking your attitude was just that. Talk! You haven't changed a bit, Nicholas Campion.'

The flush of triumph receded, leaving his face pale with fury. 'Which is a very comprehensive answer. Good night, Judith—sleep in peace. I shan't bother you again.' He strode from the room, closing the door behind him with exaggerated care, and Judith stared at it bleakly, feeling cold, as though Nicholas Campion had taken all the warmth from the room with him.

She turned out the light and huddled down in the bed, but the chill intensified, spreading through her in a cold, relentless tide. Judith rolled herself in the duvet, teeth chattering, but her body refused to generate any warmth. The satin slip suddenly felt like a casing of ice, and she began to cough drily. She wanted water with sudden urgency, but felt so cold she couldn't force herself from the bed to get it. She turned on the light at last and stumbled out of bed to stagger, shivering, towards the bathroom, then almost jumped out of her skin as the door burst open and Nick leapt towards her.

'Judith! Hell, I was afraid of this—for God's sake get back into bed.'

'I want water,' she gasped.

He bundled her back in the bed, tucking the covers round her, then went to the bathroom and came back with a glass. He held it to her mouth, and with difficulty between spasms of coughing Judith managed to drink some water, spilling a lot of it on the satin slip in the process.

Nick eyed the garment with scorn, then went over to his father's chest of drawers, rummaging about in them until he found some warm striped pyjamas. He tossed them on the bed. 'They'll swamp you, but at least you'll be warm. I'll go and dig out a hot-water bottle.'

Coughing miserably, Judith peeled the slip from her shivering body and got into George Campion's pyjamas. He was a big man, and the effect was utterly ridiculous, but Judith was past caring. She managed to turn back the sleeves a little, then huddled under the covers until Nick arrived with a loaded tray and a fleece-covered hot-water bottle.

'Feel better?' he demanded, putting the tray on the table beside her. He slid the bottle under the covers near her feet as Judith fought to control her cough.

'I've switched the heating back on,' he went on briskly. 'And I've made tea. Another dose of whisky in it might help—only this time try not to spill it.'

Judith drank the tea as quickly as she could. Nick relieved her of the mug each time she coughed, put it on the tray when she'd finished, then went into the bathroom.

'Eureka!' he said triumphantly as he came back with a bottle of cough medicine. 'Mother gets a cough in winter—which is why Dad insisted on taking her somewhere warm for Christmas this year.' He poured a measure into a small plastic beaker and held it out. Judith swallowed it obediently, then huddled back under the quilt.

'Thanks,' she said hoarsely at last. 'I feel better now.'

'But you're still shivering,' he said grimly.

'I'll be fine soon—I feel warmer, honestly,' she assured him, her chattering teeth detracting somewhat from the statement.

'I'll ring a doctor,' Nick said trenchantly, moving towards the phone.

'No!' Judith shook her head fiercely. 'I'll be fine once I get warm. Must be delayed reaction, or something.'

He touched her forehead, frowning. 'At least you're not burning up with fever.'

'I told you. All I need is to get warm.' She managed a shaky smile. 'Go back to bed, Nick. I'll be fine in—' The rest of her words were inaudible through her chattering teeth, and with a muffled curse, Nick suddenly pulled back the covers and slid in beside her.

'Look on this as therapy,' he said roughly, and pulled her close. 'Don't pull away—I just want to get you warm.'

Judith had no intention of pulling away. She huddled against him obediently, grateful for his warmth. And for a while all she could feel was relief as heat from his hard, familiar body flowed into hers. Her head fitted into the curve of his shoulder, her body adjusting to his involuntarily, and as the warmth permeated through her, Judith relaxed, yielding to arms that held her close, to a general feeling of well-being that was heaven after the icy shivering. For a while they lay utterly still, their breathing the only sound or movement between them. Then gradually their stillness changed. Judith felt Nick's arms tighten, heard the tempo of his breathing alter and quicken, and her own accelerate to match it. Warmth changed to heat and she gasped and tried to move away, but Nick held her fast.

'Judith, Judith, I want you so much!' he groaned against her cheek, and slid his hot, seeking lips along her jaw until they closed on her mouth with a hunger she had no will to resist. What had begun as simple comfort metamorphosed to fire and need and an urgency neither could fight after the long, lonely months of abstinence.

Blind instinct blotted out Judith's thought processes as Nick kissed her with hungry elation, his hands smoothing and stroking over her back and down over her bottom, bringing her hard against him, and Judith buried her face against his throat. Nick smoothed the borrowed pyjamas away with shaking hands, then stripped off his robe and held her pliant body against his with a relishing sound deep in his throat. As Nick's mouth returned to hers she welcomed his seeking tongue with ardour and thrust her hips against his when his fingers found her breasts and discovered the incontrovertible proof of her response. He moved his head downwards and took one diamond-hard nipple between his teeth, his fingers caressing its twin until Judith's head thrashed back and forth on the pillow. Streaks of white-hot sensation arrowed from her breasts as he paid lingering, tormenting attention to each engorged tip in turn, and she felt as though she were melting, turning liquid inside with all the pent-up desire of the past endless year, and she let out a stifled gasp when at last his invading caresses moved lower to discover just how much she wanted him.

Nicholas Campion loomed over his wife, staring down into her taut, flushed face for an instant before he slid his hands beneath her hips to lift her to him, bent his back in a practiced, lithe contortion and never taking his eyes from hers, made their reunion complete. Judith gasped at the shock and hot, remembered delight of it, mesmerised by a look of such intense desire in her husband's translucent eyes she reached out with fierce, demanding hands, and dug her nails into his shoulders, and Nick gave a hoarse cry and moved convulsively. Judith moved with him, her body answering his in perfect rhythm as it had always done. She smiled up into his taut face, knowing of old that he was fighting his desire for re-

lease, mastering his body into prolonging the glory of
their loving until at last his control snapped and culmi-
nation flooded them both, simultaneous and over-
whelming, leaving them clutching each other in
exhaustion so absolute they fell asleep instantly, still fast
in each other's embrace, his arms tight around her as
though he'd never let her go.

When Judith woke some time later Nick was still
holding her close and her body was responding helplessly to his before her brain had time to know what was
happening. She shivered at the touch of his arousing
hands, surrendered her parted mouth to his and once
again they were caught in the familiar, engulfing tide, the
experience dream-like and wordless and longer drawn out
than before, but no less ravishing in its bliss. And this
time when it was over Nick turned over and drew her
close in his arms and caressed her into sleep.

When Judith returned to consciousness again it was
broad daylight and she was alone. She shot up in the bed,
her face hot as she registered her nudity and the tangled
covers. Her mind in turmoil, she fled to the bathroom
and stood under a hot shower, then raided Lydia's belongings guiltily for some underwear before hunting
down some old jersey trousers in a polythene bag of
clothes Lydia had obviously put by for one of her charity jumble sales. The waist was a little tight, there was an
odd paint daub or two, and the legs were much too long,
but after rolling the latter up, and pulling on a pair of her
father-in-law's socks and his bulky red sweater, Judith
felt more equipped to deal with whatever the day might
bring. She slapped some borrowed moisturiser into her
face, avoiding her eyes in the mirror as she brushed
her hair.

How, she thought frantically, did one greet one's estranged husband after a night like last night? It was pointless to pretend any of it was Nick's fault. Their lovemaking had been as mutual and impassioned as it had always been. More so, in some ways, after the long separation. Their adventure was to blame, of course. Something primitive and basic had overtaken them after fighting their way to safety through that terrifying flood. But it didn't change anything. Nick was still Nick, and she was no more agreeable to dancing to his tune this morning than she had been before their baser urges had wiped out everything, including the spectre of divorce.

Judith eyed the tumbled bed in embarrassment. She stripped off the sheets and covers hurriedly, made them into a bundle and left the room, reluctance weighting her feet as she went downstairs to find Nick. She heard him on the phone in his father's study, and hurried past to the kitchen and into the scullery, glad to postpone confrontation for a moment. She thrust the bed-linen in Lydia's washing-machine and started it up, then went back to the kitchen to find that Nick, for the first time in their relationship, had breakfast ready. The table was laid for two, complete with butter, marmalade, and honey. Coffee was bubbling in the machine, bread was sliced ready to toast, the entire impression one of such blatant domesticity Judith was on the defensive long before Nick strode in, looking clear-eyed and confident and very much the conquering hero.

'Good morning, darling,' he said, smiling the smile that had once turned her bones to water.

'Good morning,' returned Judith coolly. 'This is all rather a surprise. I see you've even mastered the coffee machine.'

Nick's smile faded. He eyed her quizzically in silence
for a while, his face falling into the familiar set lines all
too quickly. 'I see. I take it your lack of delight in the day
means you're hung up about last night. Back to square
one, I assume.'

'If you mean that what happened last night doesn't
change things between us, yes,' she assured him, feeling
a twinge of pain nevertheless as Nick shrugged and
turned his back to thrust bread into the toaster.

By the time he brought the coffee pot and toast rack to
the table his face was inscrutable. 'At least we can
breakfast together before we go our separate ways,
Judith.'

'Of course.' She sat down, annoyed because he was
making her feel guilty. 'I heard you on the phone. Were
you finding out some way of getting to Longhope?'

'Yes. I rang Hugh, too. Well, Margaret actually. Hugh
was out on the farm by that time. I told her you'd arrive
there some time today, by one means or another, but at
that stage I hadn't sorted out the actual means of transport. You can ring her after breakfast, if you like. Tell her
you'll be home in time for lunch.' He buttered a slice of
toast, spread honey on it, then asked her to pour coffee
so matter-of-factly the night might never have been.

'Aren't you going to eat anything?' asked Nick as she
drank her coffee.

More for something to do than any desire for it Judith
took a piece of toast and buttered it. 'Do I take it you've
actually found some way to get me home?'

'If you mean to Longhope, yes,' he returned. 'The
roads are still under water round here, but a friend of
mine in Pennington is willing to pick you up by helicopter. He can land on the lawn here, and there's plenty of
space at Longhope to set you down.'

Judith stared at him, aghast. '*Helicopter!* But that will cost the earth, surely?'

'Look on it as a Christmas present,' said Nick, shrugging, and held out his cup for more coffee. While she poured he buttered another slice of toast.

'You must be hungry,' said Judith remorsefully. 'Look, let me make you an omelette—'

'I don't *want* a bloody omelette,' he exploded suddenly, and glared across the table at her. 'After the miracle of last night—which was pure magic for me, if not for you—I thought everything would be right between us. But no. This morning it's Miss Iceberg again! I want the rest of our life together and all you can offer me is an *omelette?*'

Judith lost her temper. 'And all you think is necessary to put things right is a night in bed together, I suppose! Nothing's changed with you, Nicholas Campion. When anything went wrong between us all you ever did was take me to bed to put it right. Well, this time it won't work. Not,' she added, striving to be fair, 'that last night wasn't wonderful and the sex the best we've ever had together. But I want more than that out of life. I want an ordinary give and take kind of marriage, a partnership with each partner appreciating the needs of the other. In our brief attempt at marriage your needs were the only ones ever up for discussion, as I remember it.'

Nick's eyes were like chips of ice. 'If you describe what we had together last night as mere sex then there's no point in discussion of any kind. I thought we were making *love*, Judith. Since I was obviously mistaken let's drop the subject.'

'Fine by me,' she snapped. 'When does this helicopter arrive?'

'Eleven or thereabouts. You'll have to go as you are. Your clothes aren't dry.'

'No matter. I'll bundle them in a plastic bag. As long as I can get to Longhope I don't care how I look. I'll return the clothes I'm wearing to your mother when she comes home.' Judith jumped up and began to clear the table, clattering the dishes angrily.

Nick sat watching her for a moment, then drained his coffee cup, got to his feet and stalked from the room without a backward glance.

Judith stopped her frenzied activity abruptly, fighting a strong desire to cry her eyes out. After a moment she pulled herself together and set about leaving the kitchen tidy for Nick. She bit her lip as she thought of him alone for Christmas, knowing that one word from her and they could have spent it here together. But that would have been as good as saying she was willing to resume the old way of life, with Nick calling the shots. And though she still loved him as much as ever she wanted more than that. A lot more.

Once Judith was satisfied the kitchen was spick and span she collected her raincoat and boots, thrust them in a polythene carrier bag and went upstairs to add the rest of her wet clothes to the bundle. Afterwards she tidied the bedroom and went down to the study and tapped on the closed door.

'Well?' snapped Nick as she went in.

'I can't wear Lydia's shoes, they're a bit big,' she said coolly, 'but could I borrow her rubber boots, please? Mine are still sodden.'

Nick turned away from the window. 'Take whatever you want,' he said morosely. 'Are you about ready to go? I rang Margaret to say you'd be leaving soon. The helicopter should be here in a few minutes.'

Judith swallowed, the very thought of it giving her the horrors.

'Nick,' she said tentatively.

He eyed her, frowning. 'What's the matter?'

'Have you forgotten I'm afraid of flying?'

'Since it deprived me of your company on my travels, Judith, no, I haven't.' A sardonic gleam lit his eyes. 'Besides, I'm the one who anaesthetised you with brandy on the trip to Paris for our honeymoon, remember?'

Judith flushed. 'And that was in a plane. I'm sorry to be a nuisance, but the thought of a helicopter ride is frightening me silly!'

'I thought you'd endure anything to get to Longhope—and away from me,' he said cuttingly, and gave an impatient sigh. 'You should have said something before. Dan Abbott will have set off by now.'

'Would—would you come with me, then?' she asked in desperation.

His eyes narrowed. 'Would my presence make a difference?'

'Yes,' she said baldly, gazing at him in naked appeal. '*Please,* Nick.'

He shrugged. 'All right. I can hardly subject Dan to a hysterical passenger, I suppose. I'll just lock up and collect a jacket and we'll go outside on the lawn to wait. Let's hope Dan can bring me back again.'

'I'll contribute to the expense,' said Judith quickly, when they were watching the helicopter come into view.

'Unnecessary,' was the terse reply. 'You didn't ask for a helicopter trip, so you're not obliged to pay for one. As I told you, Judith. It's my present to you. Here he comes, so no more argument. Bite the bullet, you'll be safe at Longhope before you know it.'

His last words were drowned by an unmistakable chopping noise which increased in volume as a helicopter came into view over the twisted barley-sugar chimney's of Friar's Haven. The machine looked like a great dragonfly as the roaring arc of the rotor blades hovered over the lawn, the down draught swirling the grass flat as the skids touched the lawn. Nick grinned at the pilot and ducking his head he pulled Judith low beside him and pushed her into the helicopter, shouting the change of plan to the pilot as he buckled the rigid, terrified Judith into her seat and settled himself beside her. After a grimace of a smile to Dan Abbott she sat, petrified, her stomach churning as the machine lifted up and up and with a clattering din rose above the treetops in the winter sunlight, giving the passengers a splendid aerial view of the Forest of Dean and the glittering flooded plains of Gloucestershire. It was wasted on Judith, who couldn't bring herself to look down. She sat, rigid, almost deafened by the noise as she stared straight ahead, her hand clutching Nick's like a lifeline, telling herself that in a few minutes' time she would be safe at Longhope, at the same time lecturing herself bitterly on her cowardice, and hoping the pilot wouldn't think she was an ungrateful idiot.

Ten minutes later Dan Abbott set the machine down with delicate precision in the fallow meadow below Longhope Farm, as directed, with the Long family and a couple of farm-hands as an admiring audience at a safe distance. While the rotor blades slowed to a halt Nick unbuckled a wan Judith from her seat, then helped her out of the helicopter and turned to face a rush of people all eager to greet the visitors and meet the pilot, especially Judith's twin nephews, Jack and Charlie, who were deeply impressed by their aunt's mode of arrival.

Margaret Long, a tall, handsome woman in corduroys, heavy jersey and muddy rubber boots, took one look at Judith when the introductions were over, put an arm round her waist and held her firmly while she tried to persuade the cheerful, pleasant Mr. Abbott to come in for coffee.

He refused regretfully, saying he was obliged to keep to his ETA at Yeovilton.

Judith came to with a start. 'Nick? Does that mean you can't get back?'

'I can come back for him this afternoon, Mrs. Campion,' Dan assured her. 'I'm due back in Gloucester at four. Pick you up here about three, Nick?'

Aware that her entire family were frowning at her in deep disapproval, Judith coloured as Nick assured his friend that it was fine with him.

'Sorry to put you out, Dan. I wouldn't have come at all if Judith hadn't bludgeoned me into it. As you'll have observed, she didn't enjoy the trip. I didn't think you'd fancy coping with hysterics on your own, so I hitched a lift.'

'I should bloody well hope you did come with her,' said Hugh, with unwanted violence, and gave his sister a black look. 'Margaret's laid on lunch for the multitude. Are you sure you can't stay, Abbott? You're more than welcome.'

Much to Jack and Charlie's disappointment Dan Abbott refused with regret, and Hugh dragged his sons well out of the way to watch the helicopter lift up into the sky and fly south over the Severn.

Judith felt like the unwanted guest as Hugh and his sons walked back to the house with Nick, the ten-year-olds firing questions at him, and Hugh making his pleasure in his old friend's company very obvious. Her

knees shook as she trudged over the muddy field with
Margaret, who, alone of the company, was regarding her
young sister-in-law with concern.

'What's up, Judith? You look like a ghost. And don't
give me any rubbish about the helicopter trip. It's more
than that.'

To Judith's horror tears welled up in her eyes, and with
an exclamation Margaret took her by the arm and set off
across the field towards the barn.

'Let's go and inspect my preparations for tomorrow,'
she said loudly, as Nick looked back, frowning. 'I've
made a start on laying the table, but you can give me a
hand to finish it off this afternoon.'

The barn at Longhope was a splendid place with a
raftered ceiling, ovens and a bar, and in bygone days of
splendour had been used for the pheasant shoots which
had been a tradition at the farm. These days clay pigeons
were the only targets at risk, and the barn was kept for
storage, except for the annual Christmas get-together of
the Long family and an occasional local function.

'Right,' said Margaret, shutting the door firmly. 'Are
you coming down with something after your soaking
yesterday, Judith, or is the trouble a different kind
altogether? What made you come running home so suddenly after all?'

Judith stared at Margaret, sniffing miserably, then in
a rush came out with everything, the letter from the solicitor, meeting up with Nick again, realising she still loved
him as much as ever.

'And does Nick feel the same way?' Margaret led her
over to a group of chairs waiting to be arranged round the
long table. 'Come on, sit down. Hugh can give Nick a
drink, and the casserole can hang on for a bit.'

Judith slumped in a chair, heaving in a deep, shaky breath. 'Nick wants me back.'

'Nick's always wanted you back,' Margaret said matter-of-factly.

Judith raised an accusing eyebrow. 'Ah, yes, I forgot. Hugh and Nick are in regular communication.'

'Nick worries about you.' Margaret pulled a face. 'I'm afraid it's taken a lot of persuasion on our part lately to stop him coming after you and trying to force a reconciliation.'

'That's Nick all over—how can you *force* a reconciliation? It's a contradiction in terms!' Judith shrugged. 'Besides, he just wants things to go on as they did before.'

'Has he said that?'

Judith thought for a moment. 'Well—no, not exactly.'

'Then give him the benefit of the doubt and let him talk to you for a bit, love. Find out exactly what he has in mind.'

'He made that pretty plain last night—' Judith stopped dead and blushed to the roots of her hair. 'I mean—'

'I probably know what you mean,' interrupted Margaret, grinning. 'I suppose Nick took full advantage of the situation.'

Judith thrust a hand through her hair. 'It's a form of persuasion he's always thought infallible. But enjoying all—all *that* together isn't enough, Mags. I've got used to being me lately. Doing my own thing.'

'Surely you could still do it if you were back with Nick?'

'You never approved of my leaving him, did you?' said Judith mutinously.

'Mainly because I think you two were made for each other. Can you look me in the eye and tell me you've been happy since you broke up?' said Margaret relentlessly.

Judith stared at her sister-in-law in silence, then blew her nose loudly and got up. 'Come on, Mrs. Long. I'd better give you a hand with lunch—and besides, I haven't yet had a cuddle with my niece. Is your wonderful young Nancy looking after her?'

Margaret threw up her hands in surrender. 'All right, all right. I'll mind my own business. Let's get back to the fray. You can give Tab her lunch—the faithful Nancy wants to do some last minute Christmas shopping this afternoon.'

Chapter Five

LUNCH at Longhope Farm on Christmas Eve was almost as festive as the big day itself, in its own particular way. And by the time Judith had exclaimed over the new walking talents of her little niece Tabitha, who came staggering towards her crowing with triumph, she no longer had problems with Nick's presence. Nick himself looked as much at home at the Long's table as he'd always done, and was so busy answering the twins' questions about the flood and the flight in the helicopter he was hard put to have any conversation with Hugh, let alone Judith, who asked to have Tab's high chair pushed in beside her so she could feed the little girl, leaving the invaluable young Nancy Higgs free to help Margaret put lunch on the table.

Judith, glad to concentrate on the demanding Tab, who was in a high state of excitement, suddenly realised she felt happier than she had in a long time as they all tucked in to a huge beef casserole, accompanied by vegetables grown on the farm.

'That was wonderful, Margaret,' said Nick appreciatively, as he sat back with a sigh at last. 'I'd forgotten what a fantastic cook you are.'

Hugh laughed. 'Cooking was certainly never Judith's strongest point.' He winced as Margaret kicked him under the table.

Nick smiled, unperturbed. 'True,' he agreed easily, just as though he'd been subject to Judith's culinary shortcomings all along, and turned to the twins. 'Right then, you two, what do you think you'll find under the Christmas tree tomorrow?'

In the ensuing hubbub from the boys Margaret and Nancy passed round large slices of pie made with frozen raspberries from the farm's summer yield of soft fruit, but Judith shook her head, preferring to take Tab from her high chair and cuddle her on her lap for a rest on the old rocking chair by the fire. The little girl settled down comfortably, her eyes heavy, one chubby little hand clutching the heavy gold chain Judith wore round her neck. After a while Judith looked up to see Nick's gaze fixed on her across the room, and their eyes locked, Judith's the first to fall as she stroked the soft tendrils of hair on Tab's head.

'If your friend's coming back to fetch you this afternoon in the helicopter,' said Margaret, breaking into Hugh's account of the year's highly successful strawberry yield, 'where's he taking you, Nick?'

'Back to Friar's Haven.'

Hugh frowned. 'But Judith said your parents are in the Caribbean.'

Nick nodded casually. 'That's right.'

'You surely don't mean to spend Christmas alone?' said Margaret, shocked, and shot an accusing eye at Judith as though she were to blame for the arrangement.

'It won't kill me,' Nick said, amused.

'But you can't do *that*,' said young Charlie in horror, his sentiments echoed fervently by his twin.

'Can you contact Mr. Abbott?' demanded Margaret.

Judith read her sister-in-law's mind with resignation.

'I could, yes,' said Nick, avoiding her eyes. 'Why?'

'It's obvious why,' said Hugh emphatically. 'Ring the chap and say you won't be going back. We insist you spend Christmas with us. Afterwards the roads will be clear and I can drive you wherever you want to go.'

For once Nick seemed lost for words. He cleared his throat. 'That's extraordinarily kind of you, but—'

'No buts,' said Margaret firmly. 'And if you're thinking any nonsense about another mouth to feed, don't. We're twenty-one for lunch tomorrow as it is. One more won't make a scrap of difference, believe me.'

'It's not really up to me,' Nick pointed out.

All eyes at the table turned on Judith.

She felt her colour rise and shrugged casually. 'Of course you must stay, Nick. If you want to.'

'I do,' he said without emphasis. 'Very much.'

There was a brief silence, then Margaret jumped up. 'Right then, all hands to the pump. Since Judith's got Tab, everyone help Nancy with the dishes, while I get to grips with some baking.'

Judith, anchored to her chair by the sleeping baby, had no choice but to stay where she was while Hugh arranged with Nancy to drive her in to Chepstow for some last-minute Christmas shopping when he dropped the twins off at the church hall for a friend's birthday party. Somewhat to Judith's surprise Nick asked to join the expedition, and half an hour later Margaret and Judith were alone in the kitchen with Tab, who was awake by this time and settled in her playpen with her toys.

'Do you mind if Nick stays? Really, I mean?' said Margaret, stamping out pastry rounds for the mince pies.

'No,' said Judith, absorbed in making herb stuffing for the two mammoth turkeys waiting to be cooked overnight in the ovens in the barn.

'Just no?'

'Who am I to object to your guest list, sister-in-law?' said Judith. 'Is that enough parsley, do you think?'

'Never mind the parsley. I just hope I haven't spoiled your Christmas, that's all.'

'Since my original plan was a day alone in my flat, Christmas at Longhope is quite a vast improvement, Mags,' Judith assured her cheerfully. 'There's one snag from my point of view, though. Apart from some bits of underwear I leave here for emergencies, I've got literally nothing to wear until my wet things dry. And those aren't exactly festive.'

'They'll be dry by this evening. If not you can borrow something of mine, and use Hugh's belt to anchor it on.' Margaret chuckled. 'And if you're wondering about sleeping arrangements I'll put Nick in Tab's room and push her cot in with us.'

Judith kept her eyes on the turkey she was stuffing. 'I wasn't wondering. Your mother and father are in the one spare room, of course. Who's in the other?'

Margaret gave a list of arrangements, with her brother and his wife sleeping over, their two sons in with Jack and Charlie. 'Heaven help us,' she added with a grin. 'Otherwise just for the meal there's Nancy and her mother and father, the Petersons from down the lane with their children, oh, and my sister Charlotte and new husband Tom are coming over from Bristol this year.'

Once the baking was done and vast quantities of vegetables prepared, Judith fed Tab her tea of cream cheese sandwiches and yoghurt, then dressed her in her snow suit and put her in the buggy to wheel her over to the barn to watch Margaret finish off her renowned Christmas table. Red lanterns and bunches of mistletoe hung from the rafters in the barn, where a long trestle table was laid ready with a green cloth, red napkins, and several spectacular table decorations made of holly and ivy. While Judith, knowing the drill of old, added tall red candles to the table decorations and set cutlery, glasses, and red and gold Christmas crackers at every place, Margaret looped garlands of greenery round the ancient agricultural implements used these days only as wall decorations, then checked there were enough logs in the fire basket under the great iron cowl and chimney, ready for the blaze which would add the finishing touch to the scene next day.

Margaret eyed her work critically as Judith wheeled Tab round and round the table to keep her happy. 'Enough mistletoe, do you think?'

'More than enough! What's next on the agenda?'

Margaret looked at her watch and whistled. 'I suggest we give Tab her bath next, then treat ourselves to a quiet cup of tea before the gang gets back.'

Half an hour later, when Tab was sitting on Judith's lap to drink her milk, they heard the front door open. Margaret grinned and exchanged a significant look with Judith. At Longhope the front door was hardly ever used. There was a lot of scuffling and muffled laughter in the hall before Hugh and Nick came in looking smugly pleased with themselves.

'We waited to pick Nancy up and take her home,' said Hugh blandly, giving Margaret a kiss.

She laughed, and waved Nick to a chair at the table. 'Hugh, be an angel and make Nick some tea, ply him with mince pies, then you can take Tab and give Judith a rest.'

Judith gave Nick a cheerful little smile. 'How was Chepstow?'

'Very busy. I met people I hadn't seen for years.'

'People were so keen on chatting to Nick,' said Hugh, 'it took us some time to get our shopping done.'

'Really?' said Margaret swiftly. 'I thought Nancy was doing the shopping.'

'I needed a few things,' said Nick, and smiled at Margaret. 'I wasn't expecting to stay, remember.' He turned to Judith. 'What have you been doing, apart from playing with Miss Long, here?'

'Helped finish the table in the barn, stuffed the turkeys, peeled huge mounds of vegetables.' Judith surrendered Tab to her father, then held out her hands ruefully. 'I hope Father Christmas brings me some hand cream.'

Margaret's eyes narrowed in consternation. 'Which reminds me. You didn't lose the presents we gave you in the flood, I hope!'

'No. I left them at the flat. I came out in such a hurry I didn't even think to bring them,' said Judith guiltily.

'No matter,' said Hugh, smiling at her over his daughter's head. '*You* got here. The rest doesn't matter.'

Judith smiled her thanks, then looked up in delight as outside in the yard the pure, perfect treble of a boy soprano began the first verse of 'In the Bleak Midwinter,' soon joined by several more youthful voices in harmony. Beaming with pleasure, Margaret went to the door, throwing it open to let in the beautiful sound made by half a dozen choirboys from the local church.

'Any requests, Mrs. Long?' asked the oldest boy in the group when the carol was over. 'A good choice on a farm is "Away in a Manger"!'

Everyone laughed in approval, then fell silent to listen to the boys. The recital ended with 'Hark the Herald Angels Sing,' after which the choristers trooped into the warm kitchen and fell on the mince pies and hot drinks Margaret provided.

Nick handed round money discreetly while Judith refilled mugs, and Tab clapped her hands in glee at this unusual form of diversion at bedtime. Before they left the boys gave everyone profuse thanks, then with one accord turned at the door and by way of farewell sang one verse of 'God Rest Ye Merry Gentlemen.'

As the carol singers trooped off a car could be heard coming down the track and minutes later Margaret's lively parents arrived at Longhope in a welter of greetings and kisses, Nick's presence apparently taken for granted as he helped unload mysterious parcels from the Slaters' car while the doting grandparents asked where the twins were and hugged Tab and exclaimed over how she'd grown.

'It's only a month since you saw her, Mother!' Margaret laughed.

Mrs. Slater dismissed this as irrelevant and refused all offers of tea in preference to helping put her granddaughter to bed.

'I'd better fetch the boys,' said Hugh with a look at his watch.

'Let me make myself useful. If you'll trust me with the Land Rover I'll do it,' offered Nick.

'Done!' said Hugh promptly. 'I can give my father-in-law a drink before the terrible two descend on him. Take Judith with you,' he added.

'No, thanks,' she said quickly. 'I'd like a bath before we eat.'

Nick gave her a long look then caught the keys Hugh tossed him and went off without a word, leaving Judith to a disapproving brother who lectured her about her hostile attitude towards Nick, who was so obviously trying to put things right between them. Before she could defend herself Mr. Slater was back from stowing the luggage in the guestroom, and Judith left the men together, glad to escape her brother's censure.

Upstairs she heard a peremptory little voice from Margaret's bedroom, and Mrs. Slater emerged from the room, smiling.

'I was just coming for you, Judith. Tab demands your presence before she'll settle down. Isn't she gorgeous? By the way, dear, I'm so pleased you and Nick are back together.' The friendly, cheerful woman gave Judith a kiss and went downstairs, humming a carol, and Judith, feeling outnumbered, one way and another, went into Margaret's bedroom to tell Tab a story while her sister-in-law changed her clothes.

When they were outside on the landing afterwards Judith eyed Margaret militantly. 'Did you tell your mother I was back with Nick?'

'Of course not.'

'She seems to think I am.'

'Probably took it for granted seeing you both here.' Margaret touched her cheek. 'Just go with the flow, Judith. By Boxing Day it will be over and you can get back to normal. For now just try to enjoy Christmas with the rest of us.'

Judith hugged her in swift remorse. 'Of course I will. Sorry to be a killjoy.'

Half an hour later, dressed in her own sweater and trousers, which had suffered somewhat from their harsh treatment, but fitted better than her borrowed plumes, Judith brushed her newly washed hair into its usual gleaming bob, used some of the make-up Margaret had handed over and slid her feet into an old pair of black corduroy slippers she always left at Longhope. When she went downstairs everyone was gathered round the kitchen table, eager to make inroads on the ham Margaret had roasted to be eaten cold with winter salad and the potatoes Judith had put in the oven earlier to bake.

Nick got up to pull out the chair next to his, and Judith sat down, her attention claimed instantly by the twins, who gave her a blow by blow account of the party they'd been to and the games they'd won.

'Pity Uncle Nick couldn't have fetched us home in the helicopter, though,' said Charlie with regret, and everyone laughed as they fell to with appetite on the simple, perfect meal.

Judith had been so sure she'd have problems with Nick in the emotive atmosphere of Christmas, she experienced an odd sense of anticlimax when she found the qualms were unnecessary. With so much to do and so much going on, with never a moment alone together all evening, Nick could have been a mere acquaintance for all the problems his presence caused. In fact, she was forced to acknowledge, from Hugh's point of view Nick was a great help. He kept Jim Slater entertained with tales of his travels, and, more importantly, listened with rapt attention to the rambling tales the other man told about his war experiences.

Hugh, who'd heard them all before times without number, was left free to bully the twins to bed, then help Margaret fill their stockings once they were safely out of the way.

'Do the boys still believe in Father Christmas?' asked Judith, handing over a couple of puzzles.

'No, of course not.' Hugh grinned. 'But they came to a unanimous decision not so long ago. Because Tab's still only little they'll kindly keep up the pretence for her sake, Jack informed me.'

'And because both of them still want a stocking every year!' said their grandmother, laughing. 'Right then, Margaret, what's left to do?'

There was very little. All the presents were stacked under the great tree in the hall; the food was as prepared as it could get without actually cooking it. It only remained for Nick and Hugh to carry the huge turkeys across to the barn and put them in the ovens Margaret had turned on earlier to receive them.

'You look tired, Judith,' she said, as the four of them strolled back to the house. 'I'll have to come back in half an hour or so to turn down the ovens, but you can go to bed.'

'You go with her, Nick,' said Hugh without thinking. 'You've listened to enough of old Jim's tales for one night. And after all you went through last night both of you must be exhausted.'

The silence that met this remark lasted right across the yard and into the kitchen, and suddenly Judith realised Margaret was right. She was very tired indeed, and knowing of old that Christmas Day started at crack of dawn when the twins usually hurled themselves on her bed, she smiled brightly at the assembled company, avoiding Nick's eyes.

'I think I will turn in. Good night, everyone, see you in the morning.' And with a general wave and smile at everyone Judith escaped from the kitchen into the hall, closed the door firmly behind her and made a beeline for the great pile of presents under the tree. Praying everyone would stay in the kitchen, she made a lightning examination of the gift tags, and found her own name on several of them in Nick's unmistakable hand, just as she'd suspected after his shopping expedition with Hugh.

Deep in thought Judith went upstairs to the familiar room which had witnessed so many of her emotions over the years: her grief over her parents' death, her teenage misery at being overweight and spotty, her triumph when she'd passed exams, her joy over Nicholas Campion. And her despair. She sat down on the double bed, staring at her reflection in the long cheval mirror which had belonged to her mother, then opened the bottom drawer in the old-fashioned mahogany chest where she still kept a few items of clothing. A fortunate habit, she thought wryly, under the present circumstances. Underneath an old sweatshirt lay a small gift-wrapped box which had been there since the previous Christmas. She'd been so sure she'd be back with Nick by then she'd worked overtime for money to spend on an expensive present for him. But he'd stayed in Australia, and convinced he didn't want her any more, she'd hidden the present and forced herself to face the fact that having made her bed she had no alternative but to lie in it. Alone.

Judith took out the box, wrote Nick's name on the tag, and before she could change her mind stole downstairs to hide it under the heap of presents. Afterwards she went back up to check on Tab, the dim glow of a night-light revealing the baby asleep on her hands and knees with her bottom in the air and the blankets in a heap at the foot of the cot. Judith eased the little girl on her side, pulled up the covers and tucked them loosely about the warm little body, then stood looking down at the flushed, angelic little face until she heard a slight sound from the doorway. Judith turned to see Nick watching her and tiptoed to join him. He took her hand and drew her outside, then led her along the landing to his room.

'I just wanted a word in private,' he said in an undertone, and ushered her inside, closing the door. He bent to switch on the lamp beside the bed, then turned to face her, looking at her in silence.

'What is it?' demanded Judith at last.

'Just this,' said Nick, and took her in his arms and
kissed her hard, frustrating any resistance by holding her
so tightly she couldn't move. Judith tried to control her
surge of response, but after a moment she gave up and let
the kiss go on and on until at last Nick tore his mouth
away and buried his face against her hair. When she
moved away his arms fell to his sides and he stepped
back, breathing unevenly, his face as inscrutable as ever.

'I just wanted to say good night in private.' Nick's eyes
locked with hers. 'Are you angry because I've gate-
crashed, Judith?'

'No gatecrashing about it,' she said breathlessly, pulling herself together. 'If I hadn't been such a coward you
wouldn't have come with me in the helicopter.'

'But once here I could have refused to stay.' His mouth
twisted. '*Have* I spoiled your Christmas?'   ·

Judith shook her head. 'No, you haven't.' She smiled
crookedly. 'It would have been far worse if I'd insisted
you went back to Friar's Haven alone. Margaret and
Hugh would have made my life hell.'

'Is that why you asked me to stay?'

'Of course.' She smiled to take the sting out of her
words, then yawned involuntarily. 'I really must go to
bed. Christmas starts early at Longhope.'

They exchanged a long, level look, then Nick smiled.
'Off you go then. Good night.'

Certain the unsettling episode would keep her awake,
Judith went to her room and fell asleep the moment her
head touched the pillow. But at some point in the night
she woke with a start, then lay very still as her door
opened and someone came noiselessly to the foot of the
bed. The room was in total darkness, but Judith had no
need of light to identify her visitor. She lay still, trying to
breathe evenly to show she was sleeping, half hoping

Nick would come to her, yet willing him to go away. Then when he did go away, as noiselessly as he'd come, she burned with disappointment and heaved herself over in the bed to bury her face in the pillow.

Chapter Six

JUDITH took so long to get back to sleep after Nick's secret visit she was even more fuzzy than usual when first light brought Charlie and Jack into her room, armed with their stockings.

'Can we come, Auntie Ju?' pleaded Jack in a whisper. 'Dad said we mustn't, but it's more fun opening the stockings with you.'

'Of course you can,' yawned Judith, rubbing her eyes, 'only pass me my sweater from the chair, please, Jack, the heating's not on yet. Switch the little lamp on, Charlie.'

'And we'd better keep quiet so we don't wake Tab,' said Charlie as he dived into bed, close to Judith. 'Come on, Jack, what are you *doing?*'

Jack was grinning from ear to ear as he handed Judith her sweater. 'What's up?' she asked, as she pulled it on.

He went back to the foot of the bed, leaned down, then brought her a Christmas stocking which was actually an elegant yellow wool sock rather different from the huge hand-knitted affairs Margaret always filled for them.

'Gosh,' said Charlie, chortling. 'You've got one, too, Auntie Ju.'

'Well, well—so I have,' said Judith blankly. 'Father Christmas must have heard I made it through the flood.'

Jack scratched his head, eyeing her dubiously. 'You don't *really* believe in all that stuff, do you?'

Judith smiled a little. 'This year I rather think I do.'

Despite her nephews' urgings she insisted they open their stockings first, exclaiming over the various treasures which tumbled out on the quilt. Once they'd rummaged to the toes to find the chocolate money and the tangerines to keep them going until breakfast time they insisted Judith open hers.

She'd have given much to do so in private but hadn't the heart to refuse. Under the bright, curious eyes of the twins she took out a pair of outrageously vulgar earrings made of showers of coloured glass drops, a little box containing four liqueur-flavoured truffles, a leather-tabbed key-ring with her initial in brass, a cake of expensive soap, the mate to the sock, and finally, instead of coins, a chocolate heart wrapped in shiny gold paper.

'I don't think Father Christmas did all that,' said Charlie, chuckling.

'It was a charming thought, whoever did it,' said Judith huskily, and cleared her throat. 'Ah! Do I hear the dulcet tones of Miss Tabitha?'

'Shall I go and get her and bring her in here with her stocking?' suggested Jack.

'Why not?' Judith smiled happily, suddenly ready to take on the world. 'Ask for some clothes for her and we'll dress her afterwards as well, give your mother a break.'

While the twins went off to fetch their sister Judith looked over her haul again, so touched by Nick's thought she would have welcomed him with open arms if he'd appeared in her room at that moment. When he did come, a few minutes later, he stood watching unseen in the excitement as Judith sat up in bed with Tab in her arms and a twin on either side helping the baby take her presents from her stocking to add to the sea of toys and wrappings all over the quilt. She looked up suddenly, and

smiled with such unguarded warmth his eyes lit and he
started towards her as though pulled by a rope.

'Merry Christmas,' said Judith gaily. 'Look what
Father Christmas brought us!'

At once Charlie and Jack were clamouring to show
Nick their spoils, and Tab raised her arms to him, and
Nick, a comically nervous look on his face, lifted her out
of bed and held her close for a moment before letting her
down on the floor to play with the cuddly barking doggy
found in her stocking.

'Good heavens, what a row,' said Margaret, coming in.
'I bet you wish you'd gone back to your parents' place,
Nick.'

He nodded. 'Absolutely. Instead of having such a great
time here with this lot, I could have had peace and quiet
all on my own.'

'You don't mean that!' said Jack, thunderstruck, and
Nick smiled.

'No, Jack. I most definitely do not. I was teasing. I'm
very fortunate your mother invited me to stay.'

Judith coughed a little. 'I don't suppose you could all
give me a few minutes on my own? Having dressed Tab
I'd rather like to dress myself.'

Margaret chuckled and scooped up her daughter.
'Right, you lot. Out! Breakfast in a few minutes, Nick.'

Instead of following the others out Nick stayed behind. 'Good morning, Judith,' he said, and smiled at her,
looking rather more elegant this morning in the new
moleskin trousers and dark red sweater he'd bought in
Chepstow the day before.

'Good morning. Thank you for my stocking. I—I was
touched,' she said unevenly. '*Very* touched.'

Nick's eyes, blue as gentians in the wintry morning
sunshine, held hers steadily. 'It was an olive branch,

Judith. I hoped we could forget our differences for today, at least, and just enjoy Christmas together.'

She nodded. 'I'm already enjoying it.' She smiled at him, pushing her tangled hair back from her face. 'The stocking was a brilliant idea. I loved it. Only right now I'd rather like to make myself look a little more festive, if you'll give me five minutes.'

'As it's Christmas I'll be generous and give you ten!'

When Judith arrived in the kitchen Hugh was feeding his daughter and Margaret was setting a tray for her parents while Nick and the twins tucked into plates of bacon and eggs.

'I'll take the tray,' said Judith at once. 'You must want to check the turkeys.'

'Already checked, they're perfect,' Margaret assured her, handing over a toast rack. 'But you can take the tray with pleasure. I quite fancy some breakfast.'

Nick jumped up. 'Can't I take it?'

Hugh grinned. 'My mother-in-law would have a fit if you barge in and see her in her curlers! Better leave it to Judith.'

'I'll have her breakfast ready by the time she gets back,' said Margaret, and returned to the cooker. 'Finish yours while it's hot, Nick.'

'She's used to giving orders,' said Hugh, resigned.

'Orders to eat food like this give no pain, believe me!' Nick assured him, grinning.

Judith delivered the breakfast tray, gave Jim and Betty Slater a kiss as she wished them happy Christmas, then ran back downstairs to find a plate of scrambled eggs set in front of her. 'Oh, but Mags—'

'But nothing,' said Margaret firmly, and sat down with her own. 'This morning you and I get a little treat. I put some smoked salmon in.'

'Good heavens,' said Judith, awed. 'In that case how can I refuse!'

'We didn't get smoked salmon,' complained Charlie, and opened his mouth to accept the forkful his aunt gave him to try. He chewed, swallowed and made a face. 'Yuck! I prefer bacon and eggs.'

'I knew you would,' his mother informed him.

'Would *you* like to try some?' Judith asked Nick demurely.

He shook his head. 'Not that I endorse Charlie's opinion, but I'd prefer to see you eat it. Breakfast isn't usually your favourite meal.'

'Margaret's such a bully I just give in when I come to Longhope,' Judith explained, finishing her eggs. 'Mm, I did enjoy that, though.'

'Aren't you supposed to drink champagne with it?' enquired Hugh.

'Not here, you're not,' hooted his wife.

'When can we open our presents?' demanded Jack.

'You ask the same question every year,' said his mother, 'and the answer's always the same—when breakfast is over and cleared away, and I've put the puddings to steam.' Ignoring her sons' sighs she poured coffee for the four adults, picked up the new doggy Tab had thrown on the floor, then sat back with a sigh. 'I love Christmas,' she said, beaming.

With sympathy for the twins' impatience Hugh went upstairs to collect the breakfast tray from the Slaters, and came down with it to report Grandma and Grandpa would be down in five minutes. With a cheer the boys flew to sit on the stairs in the hall to watch for them, and get a grandstand seat for the handing-out ceremony. When the Slaters were installed on the cushioned hall bench, Judith with Tab on her lap between the twins and

Nick leaning against the newel post, Margaret and Hugh began handing out brightly wrapped parcels, calling out the names on the tags. The twins were given some of theirs first to get some peace, though none of the gifts was costly because as Judith well knew, their star presents were waiting outside, too big to go under the tree.

Before the adults were given theirs everyone streamed outside in the crisp cold sunshine where, to the twins' almost unbearable joy, two mountain bikes leaned against the barn wall across the concreted yard.

'Wait a minute,' called Judith as they tore off towards them. 'You'll need *my* presents before you start riding.'

By the time Charlie and Jack were kitted out in the helmets and cycling shorts Judith had bought them they were so ecstatic their father warned them to calm down a bit before trying out the bikes, but there was no cause for worry. Once the boys were in their respective saddles they rode their mounts with instant expertise, and after providing an audience for a while as the twins cycled along the concreted paths surrounding the farm buildings the rest of the group went indoors to open their presents in peace.

Nick, Judith found, had made good use of his time in Chepstow the previous day. The parcels he produced for her contained a pair of brown cord jeans, flat brown suede shoes, a honey-coloured silk shirt and, as the *pièce de résistance,* a waistcoat in glove-soft suede a shade darker than the jeans. Her flushed cheeks and stammered thanks went unremarked amongst all the exclamations and kisses as the others opened their gifts, among them Nick's contributions of a case of wine for Hugh and an exquisite porcelain bowl for Margaret. Finally, when the baby was happily installed in the middle of the wrappings, tearing them to shreds, and the Slaters had taken their gifts upstairs, Judith bent to pick up the small box she'd hidden at the back of the tree.

As Margaret and Hugh began to gather up the wrappings Judith thrust the little package into Nick's hand.

'Happy Christmas, Nick,' she said gruffly, her colour mounting as his eyes narrowed sharply, a flash of light in them quickly veiled by thick black lashes as he stared at the gift. With care he removed the stripèd gilt paper and opened a small leather box. Judith tensed as he stared incredulously at a pair of oblong cuff-links in solid gold engraved with his initials. He raised startled eyes to hers, his stillness attracting Margaret's attention.

'What have you got there?' she asked. 'Crumbs, those are rather gorgeous! Look, Hugh.'

And look Hugh did, before raising his eyebrows at his flushed sister. 'Where did these come from, Ju?'

She shrugged, smiling flippantly. 'Just a little something I prepared earlier.' She bent to scoop up Tab. 'Now, isn't it time we got to work? Perhaps you'd keep an eye on the Tour de France out there, Nick, while I help Margaret get this show on the road. Our guests will be here soon.'

'First things first,' said Nick, and took her in his arms, baby and all, and Tab laughed uproariously as he hugged and kissed them both. 'Thank you, Judith. I don't know how you managed to conjure up such a fabulous present, but I'll treasure them always.'

The rest of the day passed in a blur of activity for Judith as she greeted guests and kept an eye on vegetables and sorted out arguments between the twins and their cousins and young neighbours, since all the guests in the twins' age group had received mountain bikes for Christmas and brought them along to join in the fun. By the time Hugh was at one end of the table carving one turkey, with Jim Slater carving the other at the foot, Judith was in a state of euphoria she hadn't experienced since her wedding day.

A striped apron over her new finery, the ridiculous earrings hanging from her ears, she passed round bread sauce and crisp Brussels sprouts and roast potatoes, Nick carrying plates and pouring wine, taking his turn to add logs to the fire glowing under its iron cowl as the large company disposed of perfectly cooked Christmas fare until every spoonful of plum pudding and brandy sauce was gone.

Afterwards the younger elements were excused to play out of doors while their elders took time to catch up on the news from relatives and friends, and under cover of the heightened buzz of conversation Nick turned to Judith.

'What happens now?'

'In a little while Margaret and I make coffee, and Hugh will bring out the port, and we just chat and enjoy being together for a while. Then the locals leave and the rest of us go back to the house and fall apart for a bit, and this evening we eat some more and, I warn you, we play games.'

Nick grinned. 'Games?'

'You know, charades and drawing games and so on. Silly, but fun.' A shadow crossed Judith's face.

'What is it?' he demanded.

'Nothing. A goose walking over my grave.'

'A turkey, surely!'

She laughed, the shadow dispelled, and blanked out the memory of the previous Christmas, when she'd had to put on a brave face as well as a party hat when she joined in all the festivities and games.

While Judith was handing out cups of coffee the four boys came rushing in, greatly excited, to say it was snowing hard and the wind was rising.

'Snowing!' said Margaret's sister Charlotte in alarm.

'Don't panic,' said Hugh affectionately, and pushed her back in her seat. 'Stay the night and let Tom drink some of this port.'

'Oh, but—'

'Good idea,' agreed Margaret. 'You don't want to spoil the day by a trip over the Severn Bridge in a blizzard. We'll squash you in somewhere—as long as you join in the games. I bet you're brilliant at charades, Tom.'

Charlotte, obviously relieved, took very little more persuading, and it wasn't until the day was almost over, the last game played and everyone at Longhope ready for bed, that she asked where, exactly, Margaret was going to squash them in.

Margaret hesitated for a moment, then Judith said calmly, 'How about Tab's room, Mags?'

Since every bedroom in Longhope Farm contained a double bed, this was a perfectly reasonable suggestion, but Margaret gave Judith a questioning look under cover of the general chorus of good nights as the company separated for the night. Nick, who had been out in the barn with Hugh, making sure the fire was out, came in, stamping snow from his shoes.

'Something the matter?' he asked quickly, looking from Margaret to Judith.

'I hope you won't mind,' said Judith casually, 'but I've moved your things from Tab's room so Charlotte and Tom can sleep there.'

'No problem,' he said promptly. 'I can sleep on a sofa somewhere.'

'No need,' said Judith, in the same airy tone. 'You can come in with me.'

He stared at her, arrested, and with a hasty good night Margaret dragged her fascinated husband from the room and left Judith and Nick together.

'Did you mean that?' said Nick gruffly.

'It seems silly for you to sleep on a sofa in weather like this. Longhope cools down pretty quickly overnight—I wouldn't want you to get pneumonia.' Judith looked round. 'Everything seems all right here. I think I'll go up. Coming?'

He nodded silently, then followed her out into the hall and up the stairs, turning off lights as they went along the landing to the far end of the house, to the room where Judith had slept all her life until she became Mrs. Nicholas Campion.

'No bathroom en suite with my room, I'm afraid,' she said rather breathlessly, 'but I think everyone's vacated the one along the landing.'

'Shall I make for it first, then?' he asked in a constricted voice.

Judith nodded, handing him the wash bag he'd bought the day before, and as soon as the door closed on him she tore off her clothes, rummaged in a drawer for a frilly nightgown received as a present years before and never worn, then brushed her hair, rather startled by her flushed cheeks and glittering eyes as she stared at herself in the mirror. She wrapped herself in an old towelling robe and when Nick came back brushed past him to visit the bathroom herself.

When she got back Nick was still fully dressed.

'I wasn't perfectly sure of the etiquette on this type of occasion,' he said, poker-faced. 'It seemed a little presumptuous to get into your bed without being asked.'

Judith bit her lip, then gave an uncontrollable little giggle, and suddenly Nick's face relaxed and he grinned wryly.

'You must admit it's a bit awkward. You knocked me for six when you announced the new sleeping arrangements.'

'Sorry to spring it on you in front of Hugh and Margaret.' She shrugged. 'You can always go back down to a cold sofa if you prefer.'

'You know damn well I don't,' he said with sudden heat and closed the space between them. Without touching her he looked down into her face. 'Given this golden opportunity, Judith Campion, I'd be a bloody fool to waste it. For starters,' he added, stripping off his sweater, 'it gives me a chance to talk. Yes, talk!' he said, at the startled look on her face.

Judith shivered suddenly and nodded towards the bed. 'Then would you mind doing the talking in there? I'm freezing.'

For answer Nick turned back the covers, relieved her of the dressing gown and bundled her into bed, then turned out the light, undressed at top speed and slid in beside her. He stretched out flat on his back, making no attempt to touch her other than reaching for her hand.

Then he turned his head on the pillow towards her. 'I'd like to make a proposition,' he said in her ear.

'Go on. Margaret said I should listen to what you had to say.'

'Grateful thanks to Margaret,' he said drily. 'So. For starters, Judith, I sure as hell don't want a divorce. As far as I'm concerned you're my wife and I want you to stay that way. And if you're asking for reasons, there's only one that matters. I love you.'

'Ah, but do you love me enough?' asked Judith quietly.

'Too damned much for my peace of mind. So if you want to keep on with your job, never set foot in a plane, and have a dozen babies, I don't care a toss as long as you come back to me and let me father them.' He let out an odd, constricted laugh. 'That's what I came to your flat to say the other day.'

Judith twisted round in the dark, bringing her face close to his. 'Is that true?'

'I have my faults, Judith,' he said impatiently, 'but I'm no liar.'

Judith felt a glowing warmth spreading through her. A sensation quite separate from the mere physical fact of having a warm, male body close beside her.

'I don't want a *dozen,*' she said after a while.

Nick lay very still, then slowly, as if she were made of spun glass and likely to break, he drew her into his arms and kissed her. 'Is that a yes?' he whispered after a while.

'Of course it is,' she said crossly.

'Then why were you so hellish cold yesterday morning?' he demanded, shaking her slightly.

'Because then,' she whispered furiously, 'you were taking it for granted that a night of—of—'

'Bliss?' he enquired affably, his arms tightening.

'I was going to say sex, only you took exception to that last time.'

'As well I might,' he said grimly.

'You never said a word about my job, or having children.'

'I was ready to. Ready to agree to anything you wanted, if you must know. But having spent the most glorious night of my life in your bed it was like a slap in the face to meet up with the ice queen over breakfast!'

'I was embarrassed,' she muttered. 'I'd been so determined to stay cool, you know, once we got to Friar's Haven. But I overdid it and got so cold you were forced to warm me up in the one way I couldn't resist!'

'Forced?' He gave a snort of laughter. 'I seized the opportunity with both hands!' He paused. 'And never gave a thought to the consequences.'

'Ah! That's why you want me back—in case there's a child in need of your name,' said Judith melodramatically.

'Whether you come back to me or not our child would have my name!' he growled, and shook her again. 'But you are coming back to me, aren't you, darling?'

She nodded, turning up her face so he could kiss her. 'Why are you suddenly so sure?'

'I've been sure from the moment you gave me my present. That was no impulse, Judith. You must have bought the cuff-links some time ago to get them engraved. When were you going to give them to me?'

'Last Christmas.'

Nick tensed against her. '*Last* Christmas?'

She let out a long, shaky sigh. 'Yes. I was so confident we'd be back together by then I worked overtime to get the money to buy you an extra special present. Only you stayed in Australia,' she added accusingly, 'and I threw the box in the drawer over there and cursed myself for being such a fool.'

Nick buried his face in her hair, his arms like steel bands. 'And I wouldn't come home because I couldn't face Christmas without you! What a pair of prize idiots.' He turned her face up to his in the darkness, his voice husky when he found her face was wet with tears. 'Don't cry, Judith. From now on things will be different. Not perfect, but definitely different. I can't change